To Yoka 20/Feb
The
bg + the memory is surviving
Thanks for that Y Percy

Every Man
and
His Dog

Percy Titchener

First published in Australia May 2010
Second edition July 2011

National Library of Australia
Cataloguing-in-Publication data

Fiction by Percy Titchener

ISBN 978-0-646-53476-3

Cover Design by Jon Waterfield

Printed and bound in Australia by Griffin Press

Front Cover:
  Trajan plus M79 on APC, Route 2, dry season (John Neervoort)

Rear Cover:
  "Mooka" McDonald with Trajan, Binh Ba rubber (John Neervoort)

Down Jungle Tracks

Down jungle tracks through shot and shell,
Ears pricked high, keen sense of smell.
Our tracker dogs with care and poise,
Alert to ambush, foreign noise.
Never whimper, whine nor bark,
Their service honoured with this plaque.
No medals pinned to hairy chest,
They stayed behind, they were the best.

Anon.

From the Australian Tracker and War Dog Memorial Park, Hobart, Tasmania.

Map

Copy of original briefing map for Phuoc Tuy Province, showing The Trackers Area of Operations

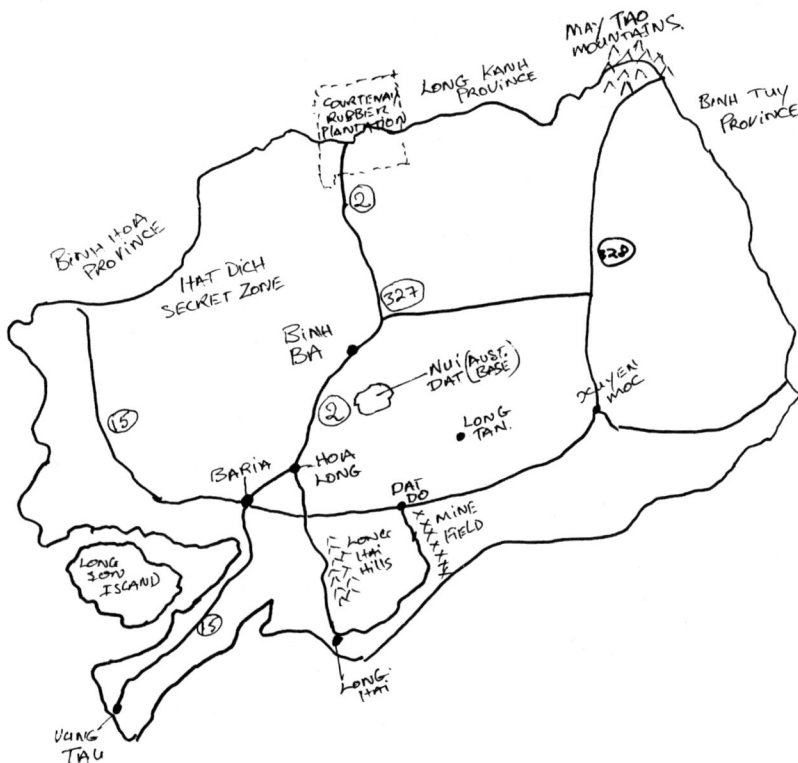

CONTENTS

Por Avani

PROLOGUE

In science, it is an accepted principle that when something is observed, it changes by the very fact of being observed and war stories are not so different. They will always be distorted and depend from which point of view these are seen, physically, morally or technically.

The passage of time adds another dimension to the memory of a young soldier, that of maturity. Never the less, as we approach these forgotten memories of war, we enter broken ground as these memories can be selective, self serving and sometimes inventive. Regardless of how objective we try to be.

To start with, the idea that soldiers in Vietnam, except the Vietnamese, were fighting for their country was ludicrous. From the moment the first shot rang out, we fought for our lives.

We wanted to live; it was that simple.

Australia and America were very distant thousands of miles away. The political speeches about serving one's country and the poetry of Wilfred Owen, "Dulce et decorum est, pro patria mori" (it is sweet and right to die for your country), was quickly forgotten or derided if remembered.

From a more intimate physical position, the view of war was formed by the job that you were doing. For example, if you were unlucky enough to have the most dangerous job in the section as the forward scout, your version of the story would (assuming you weren't shot), focus on, "Sheeit! Where is he? Where is he?" Because apart from being scared shitless, the first thing the section commander wanted to know was, "Where is he?"

The usual reply was "I don't know". After that the focus was on staying alive, looking after your mates and trying to maintain self-control; one of the fears all soldiers have is showing any form of cowardice. This for the scout was pretty hard, since he still had to try and find where Charlie was and normally that meant, exposing himself, along with the distinct possibility of being shot.

For the commander of the lead section, the focus was on deploying the section to deal with the situation. In some way the job was easier, since there was a lot to do, directing both the gun group and rifle group of the section, to provide supporting fire while the other two sections would complete a platoon attack. All of this activity for a section commander along with the application of tactics on the ground helped to control the personal fear.

The machine gunner was probably the next on the endangered species list, since he carried the weapon around which the section and platoon tactics revolved. The weapon provided a high rate of automatic fire and gave the rest of the section good covering fire.

Basically the machine gun was like a magnet for high-speed enemy metal and as the gun group consisted of three men, this made it an even more attractive target. It was well known that in the jungles of Vietnam, "Whenever two or three were gathered together, the enemy would bless them with a rain of fire".

Added to this, with the exception of the radio operator, the machine gunner carried the heaviest of loads, around ten to twelve kilos more than average. Not only was there the extra weight of the machine gun, he also carried an extra three to four hundred rounds of ammunition.

The radio operator had interesting work, being privy to all the transmissions to and from headquarters and always next to the platoon commander. At least it was interesting until the platoon attack was under way. That was the moment when Charlie would be looking for the tell tale radio aerial, which would tell him where the platoon commander was. Not only so that Charlie could try and knock out the command group but more importantly, by destroying the ability to communicate there would be no way to call in artillery or helicopter gun-ships.

"Tail End Charlie" or the last rifleman, knew that once the contact started, he had a fast run of at least fifty metres carrying fifty kilos. As everyone closed up from single file and spread out into extended line, going from one behind the other ten metres apart to side by side, ten metres apart, in this way presenting as much fire as possible towards the Viet Cong.

By the time "Tail End Charlie" arrived on the far left flank, he was gasping for air, heart pounding after running through the jungle, on the far edge of the section. Not knowing if there were other enemy or booby traps and certainly not knowing what was going on, just that he had to stay in sight of the man next to him and cover the exposed flank of the section from "who knows what".

The platoon sergeants tended to view the war from an administrative and logistical point of view since, after all that was their role. Whether it was maintaining discipline within the platoon or giving injections of penicillin in the field to a soldier whose penis "had a cold".

Effectively, there was no job better than another in the field. Depending on your point of view, the best position was probably any job in the base or rear echelon, such as a clerk in headquarters, you didn't have to put up with any of this shit, you slept dry and no one was trying to shoot you.

From a moral or technical point of view, it is very easy to make judgements of right and wrong, particularly with the benefit of hindsight. Certainly in a couple of these stories I have been critical, particularly in the story of the minefield in the "Bright Ideas" chapter. Perhaps that is because I saw at first hand, the results of these bright ideas.

It is important to remember that actual combat is relatively rare. However, the enormous intensity of a fire fight where shots and rockets are exchanged, when humans are trying to kill the other, understandably dominates all other memories.

These memories tend to emphasise the highs and lows, as a consequence, excluding the long flat plains of exhaustion and boredom between them. So much so, that soldier's memory tends to put aside the exhaustion and day-to-day tedium, which has always been ninety percent of war.

In previous wars, the battles were normally set piece and in between these battles one was able to rest "behind the line" in relative safety. In Vietnam there was no line and the stress was, in varying degrees, continuous.

More often than not there was probably no need to worry; it was just that one could never know when to be worried. However, no matter how one talks about war it will always sound bigger, more deadly and more romantic then it ever was.

War is generally understood better after the fact and like bullfighting, mountaineering and sex, is an experiential thing. It is almost impossible to explain to those who haven't shared the experience. So I have assumed that everyone has done some bullfighting.

As Willard Waller wrote in 1944;
The soldier has come to believe, with good reason, that those who talk about ideals, do not fight for them and those who fight for them do not talk about them.

Perhaps the best examples of this are the three former ministers of the Australian Government, from both sides of politics, who strongly supported sending troops to Afghanistan and Iraq. Yet thirty five years before, all three of them applied for and obtained at least four exemptions to avoid service in Vietnam. Ironically, two of them were appointed as the ministers for defence.

Many films have since been made, all with their own interpretations and exaggerations, further distorting the stories that emerged from the Vietnam War.

They could well be described as a spasm of "spam" in film culture, which sought to cover a very different reality with a mountain of fantasy.

The most well known, are those of the Rambo genre, "First Blood" being the leader of the pack, with a barely articulate, although seriously muscular, Sylvester Stallone, playing the part of a Special Forces veteran, who wreaks havoc on the establishment. This was done to punish the establishment for a range of perceived injustices, from contempt for veterans to leaving American heroes as prisoners of war, in the hands of the North Vietnamese.

Soon after, other films were made in a similar vein. Such as "Uncommon Valour" with Gene Hackman and yet another celluloid action man, Chuck Norris, who made "Missing in Action" with an acting ability similar to that of Sylvester Stallone, although rather less muscular.

While the public seemed to have an insatiable appetite for this macho myth, it should be remembered that when the war in Vietnam was at its height, Sylvester Stallone was working at a girls finishing school in Switzerland and the closest he and Chuck Norris ever got to the war in Vietnam, was filming in the Philippines.

There were other more serious films, such as "Apocalypse Now", "Platoon" and Full Metal Jacket". While they were certainly a little more realistic, they still viewed Vietnam through the prism of what would be popular at the box office and consequent profit to be made. Thereby creating the tendency for those stereotypical images of the slightly deranged vet, with the thousand-yard stare, ever prone to major psychotic episodes should anyone create the slightest annoyance.

Enough to say, that we are still waiting for the "deranged vet" to go on the rampage. Until now the "deranged vet" killing dozens of people with a machine gun, has only appeared in films. The reality of peace time massacres, have been played out mainly by high school students, mainly in the United States.

In the case of the front line soldier, for some, Vietnam was too much to deal with in the "normal" life, back in the "real world". For some this led to a life time of destructive behaviour, more often than not with a combination of alcohol and domestic violence, followed by periods of isolation and unemployment. For others who were exposed to combat operations, it became a reference point for invincibility throughout life. After all if one could get through Vietnam then there is not much else in the life to be afraid of. This also had a component of alcohol related violence, normally of the non-domestic pub brawl type of violence, with a tendency to indulge in risk taking sports and behaviour - still looking for that old adrenaline rush.

However, the reality was that the majority of front line soldiers returned home to live a relatively normal, decent life between these two extremes. Maintaining the courage which is necessary, though often undervalued, to face the problems of everyday life. Raising their families and paying the bills. In short, the vast majority of combat soldiers returned home and got on with their life.

All of the stories are written in the third person, to try and maintain a personal distance and many of the names have been changed to protect both the innocent and the guilty; well, mainly the guilty. With these changes and the passage of time, one can safely say that all of these stories could be a mix of fact and fiction, perhaps "Faction" would be the best word to use. In any case, they are not meant to be read as a definitive history of the units that I served in.

Certainly, some will recognise the situations and word pictures painted in these stories. And while all of the incidents in these stories did happen, the veracity in some of the details will no doubt be questioned. However, with the passing of so much time and copious quantities of alcohol, that would be rather like, a lot of bald men at a veterans reunion fighting over a comb.

To emphasise the rather flexible nature of war stories, I remember that while I was recovering back in Melbourne after being wounded, there were three others from my section and a

First World War veteran, Mr. Moore in the same ward. He was eighty years old and had been bombed and gassed in France. Now he was dying of lung cancer.

He was quite amazing, the way he used his tracheotomy to puff on his cigarettes (in those days you could smoke in hospital), while he told us stories of his war, broken up by rattling wheezes as he tried to breathe.

Stories which made Vietnam seem like a walk in the park. We nicknamed him "Wary Moorey" for the war stories he told us. I can still hear him in another fit of coughing bought on by laughter at his own joke. Then he would always finish with something like, "Never get too serious about this war business, you young fellas gotta learn to laugh".

After one his stories, he said with a smile, "You young fellas have to remember, that the only difference between a fairytale and a war story, is that the fairytale starts with, "Once upon a time", and a war story starts with, "Now I'm not bullshitting, I was there".

Although the years have gone quickly, the forgotten memories still return quite clearly, the passage of time allowing the stories to become less emotional and more mature in the telling.

The description of training in the army is not designed to show the army in a bad light, rather to show the type of training necessary to prepare for war. Some of the stories and notes "From the Diaries" may seem hard or cruel or twisted. That is because they are. Other stories, particularly "The Prisoner Of War" and "The Bush Scout", illustrate the paradoxical kindness and respect that develops between friend and foe during war. In a more distorted way "The Skull Cave", demonstrates a similar paradox.

The motive for portraying these stories, warts and all is to underline the fact, that if we continue to send healthy normal young men to kill other young men who live far away, then we should not be shocked or surprised if they adapt or occasionally behave badly and return home as hard, cynical, much older men, and full of black humour.

The story of the skull cave illustrates that point.

Perhaps one day we will stop doing this.

1

A FINE KIND OF MADNESS

"Madness is something rare in individuals,
But in groups it is the rule".
Frederick Nietzsche.

They had been patrolling for five days through the dim light of thick jungle, when the six man reconnaissance patrol found the camp late in the afternoon, occupied by several Viet Cong. There was always a high level of tension during these patrols, which required slow and silent movement, sometimes moving only five hundred metres a day. Their job was to see without being seen, particularly since their fighting capacity was very limited with only six men.

Once the enemy was found, everything went into overdrive. The patrol would split into two groups with three remaining as close as possible to observe the camp, while the other three would be about 100 metres behind, where they could rest with less possibility of being seen, changing over during daylight, about every six hours.

After establishing the size of the camp, exact location and the number of enemy, depending on the objectives of the patrol, they could just observe and gather information or take a more aggressive approach by calling in an air strike, or a larger unit of infantry. Sometimes a combination of both, all designed to give Charlie plenty of grief.

The atmosphere was one of surrealistic voyeurism, as they watched, while Charlie went about his daily routine in the camp, washing his clothes, cooking food, taking a pee or reading a book.

An early version of the TV programme "Big Brother", with Kalashnikov Rifles, would be a good description.

While it seemed a fairly straight-forward process, the psychological pressure was enormous, particularly at moments when Charlie would appear to be looking directly at them. It took every ounce of self discipline not to shoot. Just observing, not daring to move, that was the most difficult part of close reconnaissance. Ignoring the discomfort of a stone digging into the thigh, the buzzing mosquito, the urge to scratch or cough, always suppressed. If they needed a pee, they just lay there and pissed themselves, which wasn't so bad in the wet season, it just washed away and in the dry season, well, it kept the flies away from their faces. That was another characteristic of Vietnam, they learned to rationalize and justify anything, just to retain some sanity and above all to survive. Through the discomfort they would be trying to count the number of VC and understand the layout of the camp. Needless to say, as the numbers of VC counted increased, so did the level of tension, which sometimes developed into a truly pants filling exercise.

They had been observing the camp for about two hours, when one of the Nogs on the left flank saw George Davis the forward scout. George was the last person this Nog saw in his life and without the opportunity of an introduction. George fired a short burst with his Armalite CAR-15, which "stitched" the Nog from his left hip across and up to his right shoulder. The impact of the high velocity rounds spun him around as he fell face forward onto the ground, the massive exit wounds in his back gushing blood.

He was fucked.

At the same time two more Nogs came running towards the patrol from the right flank. The radio operator covering George fired a couple of rounds at the first one, which hit him in the chest, throwing him back onto the ground, at the same time George provided the second part of the duet with his CAR-15 on automatic firing at the second one. He started cursing as he

2

changed magazines, "Fucking bastard got away."

After lying still for so long there was almost a sense of relief that they had been sprung, at last they could move, do something, react. They ran back, to where the other three were, pouring as much fire towards the enemy as they could, so as to give the impression of a bigger force than a six man recce patrol.

Once the patrol was together they started the standard withdrawal procedure, firing as they ran, covering each other, this would go on until they were reasonably certain there were no Charlie following.

"Jesus! I'm feeling fucked!" said the radio operator.
"Not as fucked as you're going to be if you hang around here", George replied. For some reason both of them found this really funny and started giggling uncontrollably.

"Will you pair get your bloody act together and move" Screamed Eric James, the patrol commander. This went on for at least ten minutes, Eric urging and abusing them while they cried with laughter, on the verge of hysteria, with a combination of fatigue, fear and adrenalin.

Usually, a reconnaissance patrol operates a long way from immediate help and it was only once they were far enough away from the enemy camp and secure that they could set up radio contact with the Australian base in Nui Dat to ask for a helicopter extraction.

While the patrol commander was calm and his voice was rock steady, his hands were shaking. In fact all of them were at their limit, after six months in-country.

Darting eyes, twitching faces, shaking hands and or knees, like six cases of Saint Vitas' dance in a Vietnamese jungle, with no

3

chance of a chopper until the next morning. Added to this was the fact that during the adrenaline fuelled shaking they had drunk most of their water. They faced a long thirsty and tense night with little sleep, waiting for any Gooks who might be following. They had the day but the Gooks always owned the night. So they spent the night peering into the shadows caste by the moon and moved by the breeze, the darkness always amplified and distorted everyday objects. If they looked at a shadow or a bush for long enough, it would move and became a Gook with an AK47. That combined the rustle of leaves was enough to make an hour last forever, waiting for the Gooks to start firing.

After a night of this, the nerves were screaming "Come on you little bastards, come out and fight" and all the while there was nothing, nothing at all, just the neutral elements of nature at night and the jungle, nothing more, the rest was all in the mind. Sometimes that's what Vietnam was, just a state of mind.

Early the next morning, after establishing radio contact with the base at Nui Dat, a helicopter extraction was arranged for the patrol. When the familiar whop, whop of the rotor blades, sounded the arrival of the helicopters coming to take them back, the sense of relief was palpable. At the same time they were well aware of the possibility that Charlie could be waiting for one last shot with an ambush on the Landing Zone (LZ).

The helicopters came in low over the trees like huge insects, going into a steep flare seconds before they landed. The skids barely touching the ground as the six Australians, weighed down with their equipment, sprinted to the chopper some fifty metres away. The adrenaline pumping wondering if "Charlie" had the LZ set up to ambush, heart in the mouth waiting for the familiar sound of a Kalashnikov. At these moments they must have set a few world records for short sprints, this was after all a sprint to survive. When they reached the chopper they piled in, using a well rehearsed system like automated sardines they dived into their allocated spaces. Within seconds they were airborne, some on the seat inside leaning against the webbing, while others were facing outwards legs dangling in the void and all of them panting full of tension as they climbed high above the jungle canopy.

The flights back to the base at Nui Dat always gave time for a bit of reflection, lowering the adrenaline level and calming down, leaving each one to his own thoughts. As the LZ faded into the distance, that familiar feeling of relief and "invincibility" came back. "Maybe it wasn't so risky, not such a big deal after all" thought the radio operator as the tremor in his hands settled down. He couldn't help thinking how often major changes in his short life had occurred through an impulsive decision. At least that's how he finished up sitting in the doorway of a helicopter, with a spectacular view as they flew over the Vietnamese countryside in 1970.

It all started, two days after he turned seventeen and walked into the army recruiting centre. Having successfully failed university entrance exams, but graduating with honours in rugby, beer drinking, smoking and losing his virginity, more than once, the army seemed a reasonable idea. At least there were lots of adventure courses and sports, like climbing, parachuting and diving. There was also a serious war on in Vietnam, which to a naïve 17 year old seemed pretty adventurous stuff. Not only that, but the Recruiting Sergeant who he had seen a couple of times before seemed a really good bloke.

"You going to sign up today?" the Recruiting Sergeant asked, recognizing him from previous visits and without pausing once again started extolling the virtues of army life. After about half an hour, a naive seventeen year old was filling out the army enlistment papers.

The pre-requisite for the entry into a fine kind of madness.

2

DEVOLVING

Coming into the army was like stepping into a different world, an organisation totally disconnected from the civilian world. The words civilian and civilised have the same root and the business of war is never civilised. There has always been a requirement for the potential soldier to devolve.

It was and still is difficult to convince civilised teenagers, to join an organisation that uses killing and maiming as the solution to a problem. Particularly when "The Problem" is thousands of kilometres away, as it was in Vietnam. With this in mind the army had no option but to adopt a two faced approach to recruiting young soldiers. Not with malice intended but rather to make this a more palatable career choice.

The nice face was the user-friendly external civilian face seen as the protector of all, against foreign invaders who have always been on their way, but in Australia's case never set foot on our shores. The other internal face however, was like the sergeant's face, just two inches from one of the recruits. The very same sergeant who, a week earlier, had been so effusive in his praise of the army. Not to mention very considerate in his attitude towards the recruits who signed to join the army.

The hapless recruit tried to move back and the Sergeant screamed, "What the fuck do you think you are doing DRUT?" He could feel the words raining down on him, literally, as small pieces of spittle spattered over the recruits face. The recruit could see every detail of the Sergeant's mouth, from the large dark metal fillings in his lower molars to that little wobbly thing up the back of his throat, known as the epiglottis. Small black hairs protruded from his nostrils as he exhaled. This was a human pit bull.

"Do you know what a DRUT is?" He asked, as his epiglottis wobbled again.

"Umm, well no sir" he replied, thinking this was the first time he had a close up view of a psychopath.

"Don't you ever call me sir, you call me Sergeant, right?" screamed the sergeant as his face turned a deeper shade of red.

"Yes Sir…um sorry Sergeant"

By now he realised that his "friend", the recruiting sergeant had to be partially deranged, as his gimlet eyes took on a red tinge.

"For your information, a DRUT is a Dickhead Recruit Undergoing Training, Ya got that?"

"Yes Sergeant, but I thought…"

"You're not paid to think, you're paid to do what you're told, got that?"

He then continued with an unforgettable oxymoronic, "And just remember, you work as a team, you are all unique, just like everyone else, is that clear!"

"Yes Sergeant", the recruits screamed in unison.

This was probably just the sort of training required to prepare young men to travel some 10,000 kilometres away and kill other young men who they never knew. The concept of breaking down a civilian and making a soldier is the reverse of civilised evolution. This has been used in a conscious and formalised way, since the first training manuals were written during the development of the Roman Military, more than two thousand years ago. From childhood to adolescence young men have been taught the rules of civilised society, where violent behaviour was unacceptable and punished accordingly.

8

Now, suddenly at seventeen or eighteen years of age, they entered a world where they would be taught and get paid, for the most extreme forms of violent behaviour. A world in which the object of the exercise was to make the other bastard die for his country.

Not only that, but for some if they became very good at this process, there was the reward of promotion and medals.

Effectively, their training was designed to have them devolve to a more primitive form of behaviour. This would in turn allow them when needed, to kill without compunction, touching that primitive part of man's soul, which has never really been extinguished in modern society. For those who were going to Infantry, this process of devolution from a civilised adolescent to wild savage was an obvious necessity in the preparation for war, particularly for jungle warfare. Which was nearly always fought at close quarters, where the killing was very much "In your face"?

The system for doing this was well refined over centuries, adopted from the Romans by the British centuries earlier and concentrated on highly disciplined automatic obedience to orders and systems. This was developed initially, by long hours of drill in platoon formations, with the emphasis on team work.

For Australian soldiers undergoing training, the first three months were normally spent at "Kapooka", located in country New South Wales. The quarters were comfortable, consisting of barracks with four soldiers per room. Usually the days started at 6am, preparing equipment and rooms for inspection with a few minutes for breakfast.

The beds, gear and cupboards had to be laid out according to a specified system, to the nearest 2 or 3 centimetres. This was measured and any item out of alignment would result in the whole lot being tipped out onto the floor. Repeated infringements would result in the other roommates being given some form of extra duty, a form of group punishment designed to place maximum pressure on the "offender" and instil teamwork. This was done on a systematic basis.

During the day they did hours of drill during which the corporals and sergeants would scream at them and dish out push-ups or extra duties for the slightest infringement. Between the drill lessons, there were weapon and field craft lessons, 10 kilometre runs and the obstacle course. In the evening they had theory lessons such as map reading and navigation, which would finish by 8.00pm, allowing them a couple of hours to prepare for the next day before falling into bed exhausted.

This system of continuous physical and mental pressure, always with the interest of the group coming first, continued all the way through to platoon and company level, which included a prize at the end of the course, for the best platoon. The mantra was "No Jack men allowed" (i.e. the attitude of "Fuck you Jack, I'm ok") this was not only prohibited but severely punished. Whilst teamwork was the aim, the task and the team were paramount.

Unfortunately the effect was often the opposite, as a survival of the fittest mentality developed. That "Titanic Mentality", which says, "Women and children first... after me!"

After a couple of weeks, the deranged recruiting sergeant seemed positively nice, compared to the instructors. Some of whom were quite descriptive in their language when the new recruits made mistakes. On one occasion when someone dropped a rifle, the corporal was literally foaming at the mouth.

"That rifle will save your life one day; you do that again soldier and I'll rip your head off and shit in the hole!"
"But..."
"Don't you fucking "but" me lad, take your rifle in your right hand and hold your crotch with the left. Now say after me":
    "This is my rifle, this is my gun",
    "This is for fighting, this is for fun".
The stunned recruit recited word for word.
"Good, now you won't do that again, will you?"

"No Corporal"

"Good, 'cause if you do, I'm going to drill a two inch hole into your head and get a mad dog to fuck some sense into you!" he continued smiling, "and the rest of you snot gobbling little DRUTS won't forget this, will you?"

"No Corporal", they screamed back.

Maybe the army ran a course on creating such descriptive language or perhaps it was just the natural process of devolving. After all, devolving must require some degradation. Much of the practical training also had a desensitising component. During rifle shoots, all the targets were in the outline form of a human. The same applied to bayonet practice, which was done fairly often and always with stuffed dummies shaped like a human. This was supposed to be for the practice of something that was rarely used in modern warfare. Never the less it was an excellent method for desensitisation and the development of an automatic aggressive response, necessary in close quarter jungle warfare.

During initial training, there were more than a dozen derogatory and racist names used to describe the Vietnamese. It was another way to dehumanise the enemy and obviously necessary if some of them would be required to kill and fight a war against them. There is no doubt that their basic training, while quite extreme by today's standards, would give them the best preparation possible for Vietnam.

After about six weeks there was a transition period as the instructors started to ease up on the pressure and give a bit of encouragement. The stress levels were graduated over the initial weeks so that by the end they were close to levels which they would experience in the next level of training. When they had completed basic training they would move onto the next phase of training. This depended on which part of the army they were sent to, after an interview with a selection panel.

Anyone who asked for infantry had an interview of a couple of minutes, probably to ensure they were not completely insane, while the others had more searching interviews. In spite of this there were many who by any form of logic should have been sent to where their technical skills could have been utilised. However, in typical army style, someone who was a radio technician would be sent to catering corps to become a cook while a qualified chef would be posted as a truck driver. There seemed to be no rhyme or reason but one thing was certain, anyone who wanted infantry was rarely refused. For those who went to infantry, there was a near certainty that when they finished their training, they would be posted to an exotic South East Asian location.

By the time they started their Infantry training they had devolved to a stage where there was an unquestioning obedience to orders and a total commitment to the task and the team. There was no question of right or wrong, better or worse, just get the job done and the team comes first.

The issue that was always confronted openly was the stated role of Infantry which was; "To close with and kill or capture the enemy in any kind of terrain in any kind of weather, day or night". This was often stated and it was done in a way, which reinforced just how good they were and anyone who was not a member of the infantry, was by definition a lesser being. They never had to suffer the hardship and deprivation of the infantry soldier. Training concentrated on living in the bush, field craft, navigation, communications, section and platoon tactics and weapon training. Out of twelve weeks they spent at least eight in field.

Vietnam was the focus and only Vietnam. Nearly all the instructors had served in Vietnam and were familiar with place names like Long Tan where D Company 6RAR took on a battalion plus of VC. Other names like Khe San or "Hamburger Hill" where many Americans died, brought home some of the reality of war.

The rationale in infantry training was not a matter of mindless discipline but based on experience. So that the trainees could develop the capacity to deal with Charlie, as well as fundamental need to survive. Everything action or tactic was explained with; "If you don't do this Charlie will get you", which was probably right. Mr. Charles was fighting to win a brutal, exhausting and dirty war and if sometimes the instructors seemed heartless and brutal, it was probably because they really did care. They knew, they knew very well, that it was necessary to touch the extremities of all the senses to have the best chance of surviving Vietnam. While their job was to give the best that they could.

Infantry training was designed to bring out the primitive instinct necessary to survive, which exists in everyone. With this in mind, section tactics and contact drills were repeated day after day until every movement became an automatic response, instantaneous and instinctive.

In all of this, there was the indoctrination that all Vietnamese were bad, they were "Slopes, Gooks, Fish Heads, Nogs, Cong, Dinks", all names designed to degrade and dehumanise. This along with the stories of booby traps, punji pits, young children being used to lure Australians into a false sense of security prior to launching a bomb, all so that the killing became more acceptable.

At the same time, they were told how important it was to "Win Hearts And Minds", a program known as WHAM, an unfortunate acronym that was probably more indicative of the army's real feelings, rather than any true love of the Vietnamese.

Many of the new recruits could see themselves as following their father's footsteps, who had fought in the Second World War, or perhaps as another version of ANZACs, their grandfathers, who had fought in Gallipoli and France during the First World War.
In fact, one part of the Australian task force was known as the ANZAC Battalion, which included two companies of New

Zealand Infantry. This was, 6RAR/NZ (ANZAC) Battalion which served with great distinction at the battle of Long Tan in 1966, returning for a second tour of duty in 1969/70.

It was to this battalion that some of the trainees were posted after they had completed their training in the beginning of 1968. The battalion had recently returned from Vietnam and was in the process for preparing for a return to Vietnam within the next year. All of the specialised platoons such as Mortars, Pioneers, Signals and the Trackers would spend the next twelve months undergoing a fairly complex series of training modules.

In the case of the Trackers this was complicated further by the multi faceted nature of their work. The Trackers were in fact the Anti-Tank Platoon; a hangover from the days when that was their only role. As usual, the army decided to place the dogs and their handlers into the platoon and leave it with the old name. All members of the Tracker Platoon would be required to qualify as visual trackers, followed by integrated training with the tracker dogs. In addition they were trained for reconnaissance patrolling in small six man patrols, which would become one of their primary roles. The Anti-Tank weapons became very much a secondary role and would only be used for protecting the Fire Support Bases (FSBs)

The Trackers were also configured differently to enable them to operate in small groups of six to ten men, each section with a radio, which in those days was unheard of. The platoon commander reported directly to the commanding officer of the battalion, which was necessary, due to the variety of tasks assigned to the Trackers. Not the least of which, was that the C.O. had a strong interest in rugby and at one stage, more than half of the battalion rugby team were members of the Trackers. This allowed rugby training to take place on a regular basis, even through the gruelling schedule of exercises, without disrupting the other platoons. It also led to the Trackers occasionally being called "The Rugby Platoon".

Over the next months, the Trackers were able to enjoy hours of dehydration and discomfort while bush walking in the sweltering heat of the Townsville summer. During the wet season they would spend long wet nights learning how to enjoy sleeping in puddle. An important element of training was to develop the capacity to deal with discomfort and there is no doubt that the instructors were as tough as any.

With all that had gone on before, combined with their personal histories and motivations, when they finished their training, the young soldiers were ready.

They had devolved, not in a thinking or deliberate way or even in a negative way, but rather through necessity. The necessity to survive, either in the army system or when they would arrive in Vietnam.

The corporals, the sergeants and the officers, had given them the tools to survive and they were probably as well prepared as anyone could be, for the unknown "adventures" both good and bad, that lay ahead.

3

INITIATION

The battalion was to be transferred from Townsville in Northern Australia to Vietnam, using an old aircraft carrier called the HMAS Sydney, although it was better known as the "Vung Tau Ferry". Named after the port city and old French resort in the South of Vietnam, which would be their final destination.

The week before departure was filled with last minute packing, issuing of kit and final medical exams, which included an update of any shots that were required. All of this frenetic activity was interspersed with any number of drunken farewell parties held by both military and civilians who had formed friendships during the preceding months in Townsville.

Naturally some of these friendships were of a more intimate nature and a large number of the soldiers couldn't help but take advantage of the situation to consummate some of these relationships with lines like, "Hey, you know that sometimes, I don't know if I am going to make it back in one piece or not". While there may have been some truth in the remark, there was no doubt that for most young soldiers with a libido the size of Paraguay, it was a shameless, often successful attempt to have the girl engage in some horizontal folk dancing.

Finally after the last goodbyes were said amidst the tears and anxious hugs, the Trackers were transferred to the old aircraft carrier, on which they made their way slowly up the coast towards Vietnam.

As they passed through the Indonesian archipelago orders were given for a completely tactical convoy, which meant no lights could be shown on deck and all naval personnel were deployed to their guns. For most, this seemed quite bizarre, given that they were in international waters and the North Vietnamese had absolutely no capacity to attack the destroyers guarding the convoy. Not to mention that the convoy was more than 2000 kilometres from Vietnam.

Although this was typical of the over dramatisation indulged in by units, such as the "Vung Tau Ferry", who never saw action. At least they would have plenty of practice, searching grim faced, for Vietnamese attackers as they passed the Indonesian resort island of Bali. Not to mention the odd "war story" for the folks back home.

Arrival in Vung Tau was however, a rather different experience with the realisation that The Rolling Stones and The Beach Boys would be replaced by a very different sound track for the next summer. The sounds of helicopters and occasional jets screaming low overhead playing the lead and the almost continuous crump of mortars, providing the rhythm, leaving the artillery to provide the bass.

Amongst all of this as soon as they disembarked, they were transferred from Vung Tau to their base at Nui Dat by either helicopter or truck. When they arrived at Nui Dat, as they jumped off the helicopters and trucks, the soldiers from the unit they were replacing would climb aboard. They were impatient to get aboard HMAS Sydney and go home.

Of course there was the intoxicating, for the newly arrived, scent of war interlaced with the smell of a totally new country and culture. This was made all the more acute after ten days aboard the Sydney, breathing the clean ocean air. The smell of cooking from the roadside food stalls if they were transferred by road or the smell of fuel from the helicopters if they were transferred by air. The ambience was full of adrenalin.

Moving into Nui Dat, for the Trackers there was nothing new to be found. In some way, everything was second hand. The six-man tent, the bed, the cupboard, the chairs and table, all freshly vacated by those who had completed their tour of duty. Never the less the previous occupants were kind enough to leave the pin up pictures, from old editions of Playboy in place for others to enjoy.

Someone's three hundred and sixty fifth day had become some one else's first day. So the cycle would begin all over again. Little doubt that some of the new arrivals were a little disconcerted, particularly when some of them saw the hastily scrawled notes left on the table by their predecessors, with phrases such as "Vietnam—Life is not for everyone, but just remember, you are all in this alone!" The overwhelming sense of isolation was heavily underlined and with this introduction the Trackers prepared for their first operation.

The names used by the Australians for their operations were almost always low key, as were the names for their units and operational bases. While the Americans were full of bravado with names like "Operation Rolling Thunder" or "Iron Fist" the first major operation that the Trackers would take part in was called "Lavarack" named after their barracks in Queensland.

As for the Viet Cong, they came up with names for their units and locations that sounded positively sinister. For example the C41 Chau Duc Company located in the Hat Dich Secret Zone. Alongside them there were the troops from Special Region 4 or SR4 Troops.

Even the Viet Cong mail system sounded threatening. While the Australians had the Battalion Post Office, Charlie had (this is no joke, the Kiwis shot one of them), "The C195 Company, special delivery section of the MR7 Postal Unit".... "Reporting for duty sir!" Phew! It sounded a bit daunting, when compared to the best the Trackers could come up with, which was the rather bland "Trackers", from "The Dat", certainly nothing special or secret.

After a lengthy briefing, which covered every possibility that Charlie could come up with, from mines to machine guns and punji pits to booby traps, the Trackers set out on their first search and destroy operation with a sense of curious anticipation.

The small hill, which was "Nui Dat", receded into the clouds of red dust thrown up by the eleven ton armoured personnel carriers (APC's) they sat on, charging through rubber plantations and small villages. Scattering dogs, chickens, pigs and people as they raced along. They were young and invincible with tanks, mortars, artillery, helicopters, bombs, napalm, everything. If anyone was going to get hurt, it could only be Charlie, with his black pyjamas and dated equipment.

The villagers gave them expressionless stares; they had seen it all before. As things unfolded in the weeks ahead, there would be the realisation that while the Australians had control of the day, coming and going as they pleased, destroying and disrupting the daily life in the villages, the night belonged to Charlie, who controlled the game. For the people living in the villages there was not much hope, they were between the VC hammer and the foreign anvil. What ever they thought of the Australians it certainly could not have been good.

In the beginning, the Australians really did see themselves as liberators, doing something good, preserving "Democracy", winning hearts and minds, truly believing their own propaganda. Communism had to be stopped.

There was the novelty of their first operation, which gave a sense of anticipation to everything they did. After all, some of them had spent nearly two years training for this. Finally, here they were, adjusting to life in a foreign country, at war with itself and half a dozen other countries.

The atmosphere was the beginning of an addiction for some. The feeling of imminent danger, artillery, mortars, and helicopters; the continual sounds of war as they raced along red dirt roads between lush green rice paddies. The smell of Vietnamese food and smoke from the wood fires as they passed through the villages, all of this combining to overwhelm the senses. It was, for the young soldiers,

20

in a word, awesome, a real adventure. Of course there had not yet been a shot fired in anger.

Their arrival at Fire Support Base (FSB) Virginia was something of an anti-climax. The "insertion phase", had gone off without a hitch, further adding to their sense of invincibility.

They had been in Vietnam for nearly three weeks without a single enemy contact or fire fight, so where was Charlie? Eventually this would become a daily question. Yes, they all looked the same and from this came the realisation.... So who was the enemy? How do they tell friend from foe? None of them seemed happy to see foreign soldiers, with the exception of some children who would call for sweets or cigarettes. Maybe all of them are the enemy, maybe none.

It wasn't long before they understood that the only certainty in Vietnam was a definite maybe. Maybe you make it, maybe not. Maybe there would be a water re-supply, maybe not. Maybe there would be some mail, maybe not, everything was a maybe and if it didn't workout then "Sin Loi baby", "Sorry about that". Perhaps momentarily, some thought maybe "The enemy is us", but that thought was quickly brushed aside.

Two days later the Trackers were sent on their first patrol, which was to set up a night ambush on a track junction about two "clicks" or about two thousand metres, to the South of their fire support base. After the briefing, they set off at about three in the afternoon carrying enough food for 24 hours and loaded up with ammunition, hand grenades, Claymore mines and trip flares.

In the first of what would be many such nights, they had perhaps two hours sleep as they took turns, waiting for Mr. Charles, who never came. Until finally in the morning they returned to the fire support base, tired and irritable with a day's work yet to be done. It would be like this for nearly a month, every second night on ambush patrol, regardless of weather, which became seriously uncomfortable with the arrival of the rainy season, about half way through the first operation.

21

Of course the word "rainy" sounds quite friendly and given the heat of Vietnam, to the newly arrived it could sound positively refreshing, perhaps even pleasant, in the hot afternoon sun. The season is also known as the wet, which is a more realistic description, although even that is very much an understatement.

Sometimes it rained continuously. However on most days it rained between midday and five o'clock. Even the word rain can't begin to describe the daily deluge, which always sounded like a giant piece of Velcro being pulled apart for two or three hours. Worse still, far from any cooling effect, it created a level of humidity equivalent to patrolling in a Turkish bath carrying fifty kilograms and a rifle.

Everything was soaking wet, even the cigarettes and so called "water proof" matches, on the cover of which some cynical bastard had printed, "will not light when wet". This not only took away the small comfort of a cigarette but also the possibility of a cup of coffee.

Of course the war still had to be fought. Mr. Charles didn't take any holidays so the patrolling continued, bent over ducking down to avoid overhanging branches and the red ants that were nearly always there. The other reason for leaning slightly forward was to try and stop that uncomfortable sensation when water would trickle down the spine, for no matter how wet they were, that feeling of water running down the spine was quite disconcerting.

If it wasn't the rain, it was knee-deep water in paddy fields or crossing flooded creeks, slipping and sliding in the mud on the other side. At the end of the day, the few hours of sleep would be on the wet ground. Since, to remain less of a target, there was rarely the possibility of putting up a tent on patrol. They would just wrap themselves up in the tent and lay on the ground, preferably a sloping section, to avoid waking up in a puddle.

Added to these miseries were there skin conditions that developed after days of being continuously wet. Crutch rot and foot rot being the most common, which led to many not using underwear or socks. It did help, even if walking without socks was hard on the feet. Finally, there were two insignificant creatures whose effect was a hundred times more than their size, the mosquitoes and the leeches.

The evening gave no respite to any of this, with the arrival of mosquitoes by the squadron. Their high-pitched buzzing, which gave the impression they were flying in formation ready for bombing runs, which only added to the psychological discomfort as one waited for the mosquito bite.

However there was repellent which was good. The only problem was that after two or three hours the effect would wear off and one would wake up covered in mosquito bites. So another application would give another couple of hours sleep. Unfortunately years later this highly effective repellent was so good that it was banned for use by humans due the carcinogenic side effects.

More seriously, mosquitoes meant there was the strong possibility of contracting malaria, a condition that every soldier dreaded. When the brain would fry, with a temperature sometimes in excess of forty one degrees and the body would feel frozen, with veins than ran like rivers of ice. Death could seem a very reasonable option.

The second creature was the leech, the little black bastards. Well they were little to start with. However, once they attached themselves to any part of the body they would swell to many times their original size, after feeding on fresh blood. In the end they looked like a huge fat black cigar. The only way to get rid of these black "suckers" was either with salt or the burning end of a cigarette. Sometimes it seemed that the soldiers were sharing more of the cigarettes with the leeches than they were smoking themselves.

For some the leeches became the most hated creature on earth. They were seen as disgusting, loathsome things that continually attached themselves to any exposed flesh. If there was no exposed flesh, they displayed an innate capacity to find a way past buttoned down sleeves or even knee bands or ties, which some soldiers used to prevent the leeches getting past the knees.

There was a check at regular intervals, whenever there was a ten or fifteen minute break from patrolling, they would check crotch and armpits first, the two favourite places for leeches.

Obviously it was quite hideous for the soldiers to find these swollen black cocoons hanging from their flesh. Even after these disgusting cocoons were removed, they would leave an open sore, which nearly always became infected and needed a couple of weeks to cure.

Leech paranoia was further developed with lurid stories of soldiers who had to be "medivac'd" after a leech had crawled up into the penis, swelled up and died causing serious infection. The leeches did however provide a distraction from the rain when a leech victim would find one and place a small stick through one end to the other and watch the leech writhe on the ground. Sweet revenge.

Lastly, amongst all these ailments there were always a couple of days when one would be overcome by the some form of gastric malfunction, bacterial or parasitic. This would lead to a sudden leap into the bushes, followed by a sound which one normally associates with cappuccino machines, interspersed with the moans that come with stomach cramps.

Whatever the case, all of these distractions led to one thing, monotonous and absolute exhaustion; on operations the soldiers were lucky to get more than four hours sleep a night. Perhaps it was this lack of sleep that kept Australian infantrymen sane. After all, sometimes they were so tired they didn't give a shit any more, even if this attitude could lead to a couple of instances of natural de-selection. The fact that this type of natural de-selection was very rare was due mainly, to some luck combined with the quality of leadership displayed by most of the officers and NCO's.

The same could not be said of the American commanders, who often seemed to leave their platoons looking like a bunch of envelopes without an address. This resulted in the high incidence by their soldiers, of "Fraggings" with hand grenades to kill their officers, drug use and refusal to go out on patrol. Although perhaps, refusing to go out on patrol was understandable.

4

DUMB IDEAS

(When one is new)

The Trackers had been in country about three months, when they were sent in to establish another battalion FSB. The third month was regarded as the transition phase from being new to being effective. As with all transitions in war, the learning curve was steep and dangerous, requiring a deal of good luck to avoid casualties. They were sent in by helicopter as part of what the army calls "The Insertion Phase".

Like many things in war, it sounds sexual and in some way has a similar effect to those initial sexual experiences. Anticipation, fear of failure, increased heart rate, heavy breathing, flared nostrils, increased sense of awareness as one enters the unknown. Unfortunately at the end of all this, they finished up lying on the ground in a patch of bamboo instead of the alternative.

There was always an increase in tension as they approached the LZ. The last few seconds were always the worst as the helicopter flared with all of the weapons pointing outwards waiting; those seconds seemed to last forever, probably because at that point they were most vulnerable to the possibility of an ambush.

As soon as the skids touched the ground, they poured out with a desperate thirty or forty metre sprint, carrying some fifty kilos of gear, more for those who carried the machine gun or radio. Then they had to wait and see if they would meet Victor Charlie, since he had the disconcerting habit of setting up ambushes on possible helicopter landing pads.

When the LZ was secured the other elements of the Battalion moved in. The FSB was the nerve centre of battalion operations, providing logistics, communications, protection with artillery and mortars as well as a base from which the Trackers carried out patrols or waited on standby in case another platoon needed a tracking team with a dog.

Normally they would start to dig their rifle pits or bunkers within a couple of hours. On this occasion however, they had a problem, in the form of a very thick patch of bamboo, a good part of which would have to be removed. This would normally require nearly a day's work to clear the area by hand. However one of the Trackers came up with the idea of using the 106mm recoilless rifle and after some discussion with the others it was decided to give it a try.

Calling this a rifle, however, understates how much bang you get for your buck. To put it into perspective, the artillery pieces used for the salute on Queens Birthday for example, are 105mm guns. That is one millimetre smaller. They are however, called a gun, which sounds more credible as a large weapon. The main difference is that the 105mm gun has a recoil, whereas the 106mm has four vents through which the back blast is dissipated and therefore no recoil. This area behind the rifle is called the "back blast danger area" and can extend for up to seventy metres to the rear and 45 degrees either side of the line of fire.

The idea was to place the 106mm in front of the bamboo patch and fire a single round, allowing the force of the back blast to clear the bamboo. Within minutes the idea was put into action with the gun positioned just in front of their proposed new home.

On the thinly veiled excuse of test firing the rifle, they were given permission to fire. The result was perfect; the area of bamboo behind had been cleared with only a few broken stems of bamboo left standing.

Then, about half a minute later, some one from the Signal Platoon which had been positioned just behind them, stood up and slowly got out of the trench he had been digging about twenty metres behind them. He stumbled across with an unsteady gait, as if he was drunk and said, "What the fuck was that!" …… "Shit! I can't

28

hear a bloody thing!"… "It sucked all the air out of my lungs" "Was that you?" "Jesus Christ! … What the fuck did you do that for?" Had he not been digging inside the trench, he probably would have been killed.

Not knowing that the Signal Platoon was so close to them and thinking that the bamboo was so thick there would be no danger to anyone behind, the Trackers had not checked before firing. One of the first lessons learnt by new soldiers in Vietnam, was never assume anything or if you do, then assume the worst.

On that same operation, about a week later, the Trackers came upon a fairly large system of interconnecting bunkers, capable of holding about thirty five to forty VC.

After a careful check to make sure Charlie was not around, they searched the system and found a "small" cache of about a dozen RPGs (Rocket Propelled Grenades) at the edge of the bunker system. There was some discussion as to what should be done, since they would be useful to Charlie. However, at the same time, they could not be moved due to the possibility of booby traps. Obviously destruction in situ was the only solution, but they had no C4 explosive and there was no engineer team available.

At that point the youngest NCO in the platoon suggested using a couple of Claymore anti-personnel mines, which were packed with C4 explosive and probably well suited for the job.

When the platoon commander seemed doubtful, the young NCO became all the more persuasive, "Look boss, this would be a definite goer, I mean it's still C4, just packed differently" He said with an earnest look on his face. So in a momentary lack of concentration combined with tiredness and the all too persuasive argument, the platoon commander gave the ok, "Well if you reckon you can do it, just try not to fuck it up" he said.

Under the circumstances his agreement was more than generous. Given that only two weeks earlier, while they were on the rifle range in Nui Dat the same NCO had nearly shot him, narrowly missing the platoon commander's foot. The result of what the

29

army calls an Accidental Discharge (AD), which occurs when someone is stupid enough to pull the trigger without thinking.

Moving quickly they set about placing the Claymore mines so that they faced towards the RPG's, while the rest of the platoon took cover. After about fifteen minutes all was ready and the Claymores were detonated. There was no massive explosion as expected; instead something rather more frightening occurred. The detonation of the Claymores resulted in the RPG's being flung up into the air and then rained down on the rest of the platoon. It was only a matter of luck that none of the RPG's exploded and that no one was killed or injured. The only injury was pride.

With exemplary self control the platoon commander stood up, glaring at the NCO and said, "Well, I think we can move out now, just watch out for any RPG's that might be lying around."

The main area of operations at this time was located around an area known as the "Firestone Trail". This trail was purpose built with a combination of bulldozers and the defoliant Agent Orange, creating an open strip ten kilometres long and up to 300 metres wide.

The idea was to make it easier for reconnaissance aircraft to detect enemy movement. One couldn't help but wonder at the moronic logic of this plan. Since the VC moved mainly at night, dressed in black pyjamas, they would have been nearly impossible to see in the dark.

In fact, as with many bright ideas developed during the Vietnam War, it achieved the exact opposite of the intended result. While the defoliant destroyed the upper canopy of the higher trees, the secondary growth was stimulated by sunlight, which was never there before.

As a consequence, the patrols were forced to move through nearly impenetrable vegetation, creating a lot of noise as they clambered over large trees, which had been knocked down by the bulldozers. Not only did they give Charlie an early warning with their noisy approach they also made excellent slow moving targets, with the 50 kilos of equipment they carried in the heat of the dry season.

To add insult to injury, the dense secondary undergrowth created by the defoliant, allowed Mr. Charles to cut low tunnels through the undergrowth and under the fallen trees, giving him excellent cover to avoid the aerial reconnaissance teams with the added benefit of a shady stroll.

They had just crossed a wide section of the trail and were moving slowly up some rising ground, when the thumbs down signal, meaning Charlie was up ahead, came down the line from the forward scout. The standard drill started. Go to ground, look, and listen as the tension started to build, a combination of anticipation and fear.

After three operations the feeling had become almost enjoyable, like an addiction. Like the cocaine addict, anticipating the sensation, as the fiery glow spreads through system, with the feeling of invincibility. Others may die or be wounded but not you, you are invincible, it will always be someone else.

The primeval instincts are in high alert mode, as the adrenalin kicks in while everyone tried to control the flight or fight instinct. The heart beats faster, the nostrils are distended like dogs sniffing for the enemy, the mouth is dry, kept half open to hear the slightest sound as the eyes scan the jungle sector by sector as they try to feel where Charlie is.

Occasionally, some would glance down and see a column of ants moving on the ground towards a tree, the ants seemed to be in another world and provided a welcome distraction for a few seconds.

A soft clicking sound of snapping fingers would bring them back to reality, letting them know that they are to move forward in single file. Like a caterpillar closing up, ready to swing around and form an extended line, which will place the maximum amount fire power towards Charlie. After a few minutes they were on the edge of an old bunker system, and after prolonged and careful reconnaissance, to ensure that Charlie wasn't around, they started to check out the system, looking for weapons or ammunition. It was common to use old bunker systems, fire places, graves, even toilets, as hiding places.

After two months in country the Trackers instincts and team work was well developed, but they were still learning and while it was obvious that there had been no recent activity in this system, they maintained a 50% "Stand To" whereby half of the platoon started to "brew up" while the other half remained at the ready. It was always like that, there never seemed to be the possibility of real rest.

One of the Trackers, Ian, was leaning up against a tree sipping his coffee, thinking of his recent five day R&R and the unforgettable five days which he had spent in Bangkok. Five days of sex, drugs and rock 'n' roll. A totally surreal memory, at least to a young nineteen year old soldier in 1970. He was still back there in Bangkok. That was until Bill, one of the machine gunners, came racing around the tree, his face a mask of sheer terror.

"Yaaaggghhh! there's a fucking white phos grenade" he yelled, referring to the deadly white phosphorous grenade. These combined high explosive and phosphorous sheathed in metal resulting in three choices of wounds, blast, shrapnel or burning phosphorous. Both of them hugged the ground waiting for the explosion, their minds racing through the combined potential effects of the explosive force with shards of metal and pieces of burning phosphorous. After about ten seconds Ian said, "Well, where is the bloody thing? ".

"It's in a tin", replied Bill.

"In a tin? What do you mean in a fucking tin? "

"It's in a ration tin on the other side of the tree"

Staying on the ground, Ian peered around the tree and saw a US Army ration tin upside down.

"Yeah, ok. I can see the tin, where's the Willie Pete? " he said referring to the White Phosphorous grenade.

"It's hanging by a piece of string inside the tin"

They tied some cord around the tin and moving back some ten metres behind cover they pulled the tin over and waited.... nothing.

After a couple of minutes they moved forward slowly and understood how lucky they had been. The grenade had been suspended by some cord, tied to the ration tin and attached to the grenade pin. So when the ration tin was lifted the pin would be pulled and the grenade would explode. What prevented the pin from being pulled was the coating of rust which had fixed the grenade pin to the safety bail.

"Jesus that was fucking lucky", said Ian.

At that point the platoon sergeant came up. "So what's going on here?"

After they explained what had happened, the platoon sergeant said,"Ok, I'll fix it, you fellas get back over there" He said, indicating a piece of low lying ground which would shelter them from any potential danger. They moved down behind a large mound of earth and watched as he took the grenade in one hand and pulled the pin with the other.

It was an unforgettable moment of fear, "Oh shit... he's going to kill himself," thought Ian, as the sergeant threw the grenade. Five or six seconds later, it exploded harmlessly twenty metres away.

"Well", said the sergeant as he smiled, "That's fixed".

"What's the matter with you blokes? You look like you've seen a ghost"

After a few moments Ian looked at him and said "Well the thing is, if you were going to set up a booby trap, what sort of fuse would there be, a normal five to seven second delay or an instantaneous fuse?" There was an embarrassed silence then nervous laughter as they realised how lucky they had been.

In retrospect it seemed and was quite funny. Vietnam produced many anecdotes like this, of near tragedies, which became farcical comedy. For every serious incident there must have been at least a dozen near misses, which acted like a reminder that Vietnam was a place where life always had the possibility of being a near death experience.

Particularly when one was new.

5

LOTTERIES

For all the participants and the people back home, a lot of Vietnam was about numbers. These were seen as necessary indicators, to demonstrate that Charlie was losing the war. The numbers focused on how many killed, how many wounded and how many civilian casualties. The last category generally attracted the military euphemism of "collateral damage".

On reflection, it takes a cold and exacting mindset to reduce human casualties down to a series of batting averages, although perhaps this was driven by the economic cost of all this. In 1969, at the height of the Vietnam War, the Americans were paying the then huge sum of one hundred million dollars a month.

The Americans had figured out that each Viet Cong killed cost around $21,000.00 US dollars, assuming of course, that everyone was telling the truth about enemy casualties. There was good reason to doubt the after-action tally, given the American obsession with what became known as the "kill ratio".

This was adopted by all the players and used like a scorecard. The metaphors of sport were every where, "We work as a team", "Staying focused" and so on.

The optimum ratio to be achieved by the Americans and their allies was 10 VC killed for one of theirs, not surprisingly everyone arrived at the same ratio. On some occasions, as the reports ascended the chain of command, mysteriously the number of enemy casualties increased in tandem, sometimes exceeding the desired ratio. In some way it seemed imperative that the allies were shown to be ten times better than some scrawny little guy in black pyjamas.

There were several methods of stating enemy casualties, a common one being an estimation of enemy killed and wounded, which was very useful when Mr. Charles had given the foreigners a bit of a pasting. It would allow them to convert small defeats into victories.

The estimates in this category would have been strong contenders for the Nobel Prize for fiction. Also used was the combination of, "Enemy killed by body count and blood trails of an estimated number of wounded". This had much greater credibility since bodies were an absolute form of evidence, often on display for the journalists.

Although this didn't allow for "enemy civilians" or that the estimated six enemy wounded more likely, could have been two VC, running around like chooks with their heads shot off, creating any number of different blood trails.

Another was the straightforward "Enemy killed by body count, and wounded, taken POW". Now this was irrefutable, if one was prepared to overlook the odd civilian killed or wounded, particularly since civilian casualties attracted investigation and compensation. With all these variables by 1970 it was possible that the allies had killed or wounded at least half of the North Vietnamese Army.

So who were they fighting? Ghostly shadows or phantoms in black pyjamas? Sometimes it felt that way, one or two Australians would be killed or wounded, and then "Charlie" would melt away, just disappear. If he had taken any casualties, they would be carried away leaving a few bloodstains or drag marks. This apart from distorting the body count was quite demoralizing.

Old soldiers often talk about the luck or lottery of war and Vietnam had all of that. A mine that was stood on but never exploded, the booby trap that was tripped but never went off, a missed helicopter flight that crashed, no disease after a drunken night with a prostitute. These were happy lottery wins.

36

Many times, aircraft bombing missions and artillery missions were based on the lottery of chance, rather than hard data. During the war in Vietnam, unlike today, there were dumb bombs and a few smart pilots. Mind you the civilian casualties seem to have maintained the same sort of ratio, so nothing much has changed in spite of the technology.

A classic example of the artillery lottery was the concept of Harassment and Interdiction fire. A system by which the artillery or mortars would given a piece of ground with boundaries of about a thousand metres on each side, then commence to fire a couple of hundred rounds hoping to kill, make the enemy move or cut off the enemy's withdrawal. No one knew how effective this was, although it certainly added to the atmosphere of war with the continual c-r-u-m-p of artillery fire and at night time it was like a security blanket, since in truth everyone knew that the Nogs controlled the night. In some way, for the foreign soldiers, the noise of artillery was like a drumbeat in some primitive ritual. It helped to drive away the Gooks and their evil spirits.

The Americans developed another lottery system called, "clearing by fire", which consisted of opening up on any suspicious area with everything they had, artillery, mortars, machine guns, napalm…. the lot. They used this system as part of their daily routine, twice a day, at dawn and dusk. It was very much a hit and miss lottery, mainly the latter and if there was a hit then it was a win, unless it was civilian, in which case it was collateral damage.

The irony of all this, was that many of the weapons were fired by national servicemen, who had been drafted on the basis of a lottery, whereby dates of the month would be picked out of a barrel and every twenty year old born on that date would be required to serve. Needless to say, they felt very much like losers in the lottery, the winners were back in Australia enjoying their youth.

As it turned out, in 1969, the first soldier from 6 RAR killed in action, was a national serviceman, Barry James. He was manning a machine gun as part of an ambush when two VC came along a track and the ambush patrol opened fire. Although they were hit, the VC withdrew and as they ran back one of them fired a burst without even looking, two of those rounds hit Barry James in the head, killing him instantly. This was one of the sad lottery stories of Vietnam.

In the same twenty four hour period as a direct contrast in the lottery of war, 1 platoon A Company was moving forward late in the afternoon when they found an enemy bunker system and in the words of Rick Fischer, "All hell broke loose", with grenades and automatic weapons fire. Suddenly there was a finned projectile coming towards them and Geoff Chisholm was hit in the chest with a rifle grenade. Apart from being winded there was no other injury, for some inexplicable reason it didn't explode. "Chizz" was a lottery winner.

For those who volunteered and wanted to go to Vietnam, in a sense they fixed the lottery so they had a win too….. until they arrived there.

6

36 HOURS IN VUNG TAU

"Just say you love me; you don't have to mean it"

After nearly three months of nearly continuous operations "in country", they were given a thirty six hour R & R (Rest and Recreation) pass, which was generally referred to as "Root and Rave", to the beach side town of Vung Tau. They showered, shaved, changed into civilian clothes and climbed aboard the trucks waiting to take them to the leave centre. The air was filled with testosterone laden discussions of what they would be doing in the bars around the leave centre. Vung Tau was about an hour's drive through outlying villages, weaving in and out of bullock carts, small vans and slower Vietnamese buses. These were equipped with a drum of water on the driver's cabin, from which ran a hose down to the engine. The strangest cooling system the Australians had seen, but like everything else in this country, one way or another, it worked.

As they got close to the town centre the Trackers passed groups of children, who would laugh and shout "buku boom boom" at the same time banging the upper part of a closed fist against the upper hand, which was held palm downwards. Obviously this was something sexual, then in a flash of understanding they understood almost immediately, this was a remnant of French culture , it was "Beaucoup boom boom" not "Buku". Ahhh... "La belle France, merci beaucoup"! As someone once said, "While the French may have lost their wars at least they passed on their whores".

They drove through a couple of checkpoints, where the Military Police made them feel about as welcome as turds in a swimming pool. After all, the Australian soldiers on leave were the only enemy the Military Police had and their job was to keep everyone under control.

Finally they arrived at the "Badcoe Club", named after an Australian officer who was awarded a posthumous, they usually are, VC earlier in the Vietnam War. In this case the VC was a Victoria Cross not Viet Cong. That was the thing about Vietnam, full of ambiguity and continuous contradictions. The Badcoe Club was the place they would stagger back to after an evening of drunken debauchery.

The unduly puritanical attitude to going on leave in Vung Tau probably came from the haunting fear that the soldiers might actually be having a good time amongst the bars and the women. This was demonstrated by the briefing given on arrival by a padre, who saw everything through the prism of moral indignation. The padre told them not to touch any of the women, smoke marijuana, get drunk or start any fights. Reminding them of what he called "Black Syphilis" or "Saigon Rose", an incurable strain, which sent you blind or mad, or sometimes both. It was found only in Vietnam. There were rumours of soldiers never allowed to return home because of this incurable strain.

By now his credibility gap was bigger than the Grand Canyon and the briefing had become a ridiculous farce that left everyone in tears of silent laughter. The padre's obsession with soldiers visiting the bars and spending time with Vietnamese girls only demonstrated that pornography is in the groin of the beholder and that celibacy was the worst form of self-abuse. Finally the only thing the padre achieved was precisely the opposite of that which he intended. Until he spoke, they weren't certain these facilities were so readily available and this made the bar girls seem all the more alluring.

There was always something strange about the concept of a Christian padre telling the soldiers, that God was most definitely on their side and it was not only cool, but a really good thing, to go out there and kill Vietnamese.

It was however definitely bad and most uncool, to wind up in bed with a Vietnamese girl and if they did, God would visit them with the dreaded incurable "Black Syphilis". After which they would never go home. The fact was that nobody ever contracted this mythical disease and he was probably exaggerating the resistant strains of VD, unless of course there are some blind Australians, in their fifties and sixties, still roaming around Vung Tau.

Everyone was required to attend this ridiculous harangue, after which they were like dogs straining on a leash. Imagine, after six weeks in the jungle, some 120 young men between 19 and 22 years old, who had never left home before, were about to experience the dubious delights of the bars in Vung Tau, where they would soon discover there was even more available than the Padre had described.

The first unforgettable moment occurred on entering the Grand Hotel, which had one the most interesting toilet facilities. This consisted of an old porcelain urinal, which was just below waist height. Above which was a one-way mirror that looked into a room, where about a dozen Vietnamese girls were dancing. Each girl would have a number pinned to her shoulder; the idea being, that one would tell the boy at the entrance which number they wanted to "dance with".

Now this had to be, if it was ever needed, a verification that dancing was the perpendicular expression of horizontal desire. Never mind that while looking through the mirror "the equipment was already in hand", which sometimes led to what can only be described as a "Paradoxical Pavlovian" response; that the dog trained Pavlov to ring the bell before he salivated.

The other "memorable product" on sale at The Grand Hotel, was the Four Bs for four dollars, which consisted of, a beer, a blowjob, a bong and a blue movie all at the same time! In fact for an extra three dollars you could have an extra girl. A clear example that sex for money was and still is cheaper than "sex for free".

41

Remember this was 1969 and oral sex was every boy's dream. Never mind what year it was, the concept of soixante-neuf was (and still is) illegal in many states of the USA. A girl who would do this was a rarity, to be treasured when found! Unlike today when it is "de rigueur", the "plat de jour", a mere appetiser before the main course. Yes, the twenty-some-things of today don't know how lucky they are.

For the young soldiers this was the only form of distraction available, the only place to forget Vietnam, which was sometimes called "The Meat Grinder". Anything went. There were no boundaries, no limits, drugs, sex, alcohol, and violence. They not only had their fill, they overdosed. They drank too much and smoked too much Mary J. and within twenty-four hours most of them knew every scene of what seemed to be the only porno movie in town, a flickering black and white film which these days would seem quite anachronistic.

Back at the leave centre, experiences were shared and exaggerated between them, each trying to better the other.

"Tell ya what mate, you wouldn't believe it, I had one girl licking my balls while the other was sucking me off!" ...... "Then, while I'm smoking the joint, I feel myself coming in her mouth and she goes harder...I mean fucking hell that was something else!"

"Yea, well I'm sitting up the back of this bar and these girls come up to me saying, "You buy me Saigon tea... you buy me Saigon tea and you hap blojop flee". "Well I couldn't pass that one so the deal was done in a second, too good to pass up".

"Hey guys, I'm sucking on a whisky bottle while she's sucking on me. So while her head's moving up and down on my lap, I slide my hand along the inside of her leg to her stomach then into her pants and mate, you're not going to believe this... there's a fucking ferret!" "Mate, this was a he! I've shit myself, I mean bloody hell! I was being sucked off by a guy!" He continued, "Tell ya what, I was out of there fast mate". "Zipped up my pants

42

while he/she was still trying to hang on like a pair of lips stuck to a frozen glass and by the time I started running all the heavies in the bar were screaming for money. I didn't pay a thing mate, no way! Tell you what, from here on, I'm checking them out before I go near them."

Now and then there was the young soldier who "fell in love" with a bar girl on the first day and went through the process of a Vietnamese wedding on the second day, followed by a massive hangover on the third day. Often on the second or third leave there would be the discovery that he was not the only "Husband", which more often than not would lead to an even bigger hangover.

Probably the most notorious place was the "69 Barber Shop and Steam Bath" where every fantasy could be made real, except the one everyone wanted; to be back home. For all that, this "Barber Shop" was probably unique. Near the door there were two old barber chairs which seated clients waiting for their massage "With Happy Ending".
A beer was supplied in a glass with a lump of ice in it, the traditional Vietnamese way to serve cold beer, as the drink was served about half a dozen girls would gather around the "client" looking for his attention. Often this was achieved with lurid descriptions of the services they would provide.
At the end of all this the unsuspecting soldier would stagger out of the "69 Barber Shop and Steam Bath" minus his wallet and anything else of value. After all there was nothing like a cold beer full of drugs to catch them off guard.

As it turned out, the most dangerous enemy around the Vung Tau leave centre, were the Australian military police. There was a curfew in place, which meant that everyone had to be back at the Badcoe Club by 9.00pm, needless to say there were those who felt the need to stay out longer. Returning after curfew was a tricky business because to avoid the checkpoints they had to walk around

43

to the beach side of the leave centre then pick our way through the barbed wire. Often the Military Police would set up spotlights along the barbed wire and wait for the curfew breakers.

This problem was solved easily enough by simply swimming around the wire. On the first night all went well. However on their second night, there were eight or nine of them coming back in the early hours of the morning. The combination of alcohol and who knows how many joints left them very unsteady and staggering waist deep through the water about 20 metres from the shore.

Suddenly, they were caught up in barbed wire, which had been placed by the Military Police under the water out to some fifty metres from the low water mark. "Oh shit! What the fuck is this!" they were all over the place.

This was like D-Day, a re-enactment of Normandy's Omaha beach. In a matter of minutes, they were bundled into the back of the Military Police van and taken back to the guard house where they were charged with disobeying standing orders. Military justice is nothing if not swift.

Early the next day they were paraded before the Company Commander who, in the army system is required to act as judge, jury and executioner. Within 15 minutes the offenders were sentenced to seven days field punishment and a ten dollar fine. This might not sound so bad until one understands that for the next seven days they would fight the war without payment. Making the price of a blow job, relatively speaking, one of "Clintonesque" proportions.

Daytime activities at the Badcoe Club revolved around the pool or the beach, recovering from the activities of the night before with yet another can of beer.

For entertainment, they could watch the air strikes going in on the Long Hais, a group of hills some thirty kilometres away. This was pretty much a daily event interspersed with the occasional "dust off" helicopter bringing in wounded to the hospital next door.

It was quite bizarre, as if they had a grandstand view of war, their own reality TV, along with the constant reminder that one of them could be on those helicopters. Though never really believing it, after all, in war it was always other guy who was killed or wounded.

On the third day, late in the morning they boarded the trucks and head back to their base at Nui Dat, in worse condition than when they arrived. They had raved and were well and truly rooted and probably would have been better prepared for the next operation if they were not given any leave at all.

The 69 Bar at Vung Tau

7

THE TALISMAN

In Vietnam, the smell of war, bought with it an abundance of the symbols of faith or superstition. Such as miniature Bibles, Christian crosses and small golden Buddhas. For those with less faith in the conventional, there was a wide range of protective charms to choose from. Generally items of a personal nature, which had been with an individual through a number close calls or perceived serious danger, would become a "lucky" charm or Talisman.

It could be the jungle green sweat rag around the neck, a pendant given by a close relative or even a cigarette lighter. Whatever it was, attachment to "The Talisman" became stronger as the tour progressed, so that by the last few months the owner would be in a cold sweat if he had to do a patrol without his "protector".

The few soldiers who didn't use or have a talisman, often developed rituals prior to going out on operations, such as packing their gear in a certain way, or carrying extra hand grenades or even a machete. These were like security blankets. For some loading up developed it's own ritual; first the basic webbing, then the big pack followed by two linked belts of machine gun ammunition, a couple of mouthfuls of water, check the gas regulator and safety catch on the rifle, a couple of Hail Marys and Our Fathers, after which all was ready.

Effectively, everyone had a talisman and if it didn't bring you "good luck", well it saved you from "bad luck" and "bad luck", was all around. "Bad luck" normally left one totally FUBAR'd (Fucked Up Beyond All Recognition), as some would discover, there really were worse things than dying for a young man of nineteen or twenty. Let's face it, if you have a bullet pass through your nose and take out your eye with part of your cheekbone, you get to be a monster at nineteen, a Cyclops with half his face missing. There goes the girlfriend, your family and friends will feel total pity, which is the last thing you need and it's not such a great look at the job interview.

As with many of the Trackers, Geoff developed a strong attachment for what-ever talisman they had. In his case it was a small pendant his girlfriend Janet had given to him. Geoff's aim, like the vast majority of front line soldiers, was not to win the war but to complete his twelve month's tour of duty in one piece. In the jargon of his mates, he became "Short" and the shorter he became the more attached he was to the pendant.

When he reached the point where he only had a couple of months left, he would constantly rub the pendant between his fingers, especially when there were moments of tension.

The Trackers had just returned to their fire support base, after a four day patrol, when the platoon sergeant called them out and said that one of them would be given a 36 hour leave pass to Vung Tau. Since this particular leave was an extra one, only one would be lucky enough to go and that would be on the basis of a lottery. The platoon sergeant had them write their names on a piece of paper and placed them in a hat. When that was done, the platoon sergeant drew out one piece of paper as Geoff reached up to rub his pendant with his thumb and forefinger.

"Go on, call my name out", he thought as the sergeant opened the small piece of paper.
"Right Geoff, you're going", he said.
"That's great!" said Geoff and thought, "At least that will be three days less out here", he thought, as he started back towards his tent, to prepare his gear for the next day.
Sleep came slowly that night as Geoff tossed and turned, with continuous thoughts anticipating the next three days, without the daily grind of patrolling.
The next day, Geoff stood waiting at the LZ for the Chinook helicopter, which would take him to Nui Dat from where he would

be taken by truck to Vung Tau. He reached for his talisman as he thought how lucky he was and maybe Janet was right, the talisman really did work, not just to help avoid bad luck, but also to bring good luck.

Suddenly he realised that the talisman wasn't around his neck. "How could that be?" He asked himself, anxiously, "Shit! I've had it for months and Janet will be really pissed off"

As the Chinook approached the fire support base, Geoff saw the platoon sergeant coming towards him.

"Look I'm sorry sarge, but I can't go'" he blurted out;

"What do mean you can't go?"

"I just feel lousy", replied Geoff.

After all, he couldn't tell him that he was scared because he didn't have his Talisman and that this was an impulsive decision born out of instinctive fear, rather than any form of logic.

"You realise that we don't have time to get someone else to take your place?" said the sergeant.

"Yeah, I'm really sorry," said Geoff "But I just feel like shit".

"Well next time don't wait till the last minute, we could have used that place for someone else", said the sergeant abruptly.

Unthinkingly Geoff reached for his neck and realised for the second time, that the Talisman was gone. "Yeah, that's it!" Without the talisman there was no more luck. The feeling of disappointment was palpable, as he said, "I hate this fucking place", he said slowly to himself, exactly as the letters which he had written on his hat; IHTFP!

He watched as the Chinook was loaded and took off with the usual ungainly wobble of the sling load underneath, then turned and started back towards his tent. He had walked about twenty metres when there was a change in the sound of the engine, followed by a loud crack.

Everyone in the fire support base watched in horror, as the twin bladed Chinook slowly rolled over, out of control. The back rotor had separated from the helicopter while the front rotor was still spinning. This forced the helicopter onto its back, as it fell out of the sky exploding when it hit the ground, into a fire ball of aviation gasoline and ammunition.

"Jesus fucking Christ", said Geoff as he joined the others running towards the crash site some three hundred metres away in the thick jungle.

There was little they could do. The five crew members were probably killed on impact and although one of the soldiers was able to get close enough to see the mangled corpses of the two pilots, once the ammunition started exploding there was nothing left to do, except wait until the flames died out.

A couple of hours later, Geoff was back sitting on the edge of his weapon pit, as a heavy and depressive atmosphere hung over the fire support base. He felt exhausted and lay down to sleep, thinking, "Where was the logic?" There was no logic, just an emotional attachment to a pendant given to him by his girlfriend. How lucky was that? A moment of doubt, after realising he had lost his talisman, had made him decide to refuse a leave pass. As a consequence he was not on the chopper that fell out of the sky.

But what do I do now? He thought to himself as his self confidence slipped away. No Talisman, no luck.... As the memory of the chopper falling from the sky, was played in his mind, over and over. Then, as he was drifting off to sleep, Geoff saw a silver reflection on the ground by his pack. There it was! The talisman!
He reached over and picked it up and saw where the clasp on the chain had broken. It must have been during the previous restless night. In any case, he was not going to loose the talisman again. While it was less pleasing aesthetically, Geoff placed the talisman on the thin but much stronger piece of chord, used for his Identity Tags or "Dog Tags" as they were more commonly called.

From that moment for the rest of his time in Vietnam, the talisman would never leave him.

Geoff finished his tour of Vietnam and like most other combat soldiers, restarted his life back in the "Real World". The one thing he did keep from those days was The Talisman. A continual reminder, that small decisions can have major consequences. As the years went past Geoff had the same amount of good and bad fortune as most others in the life. In fact he never really had bad luck. Was it the talisman? Who knows?

One thing is certain, even today, all these years later, whenever Geoff has a moment of uncertainty, he feels for the talisman around his neck. Mind you not for good luck, not at all. Just to avoid bad luck and in any case, as he will tell anyone prepared to listen, he is not at all superstitious and never has been.

8

THE SKULL CAVE

Perhaps it was a night of drunken bravado or a momentary lack of confidence, a way to overcome the fears they all had. Whatever the motive, they decided to call themselves "The Phantoms of the Jungle", after the comic strip character "The Phantom, the ghost who walks".

Under the circumstances it was quite a reasonable name for a section of ten men, whose job involved reconnaissance and tracking down Mr. Charles using their visual tracking skills and dogs. Whatever the reason, the name made them feel that little bit more confident. All the more so, when about three months into their tour, while on a short two day patrol they found "Charlie", which shouldn't be considered so unusual, after all that was their job.   This "Charlie", however, was different from the others; he had been dead for a long time, when one of the dogs, Marcus, found him.

His handler, Dennis, felt the tracking lead tighten as Marcus strained at the leash, "Hey, back off!" he said, jerking the lead back. Suddenly Marcus started digging.

"What the fuck are you doing", said Dennis moving up next to the dog.
"Shit! You've found a grave".

He stopped and signalled for the section commander to come up as the rest of the section moved into a defensive position.

"What have you got?" asked Rob, the section commander.
"Aah, he's found a bloody grave", replied Dennis as he pulled Marcus away from the grave he was happily digging up.

"Looks like he's found a skull", said Rob pointing to a round white object in the red dirt. "Anyway", continued Rob, "I'll get a couple of the others up here to dig him up and make sure there are no weapons underneath", he said referring to the Viet Cong's habit of using graves as a weapons cache. Once the area was secure, two of the Trackers set about digging out the grave. After about half an hour they had excavated the grave and found nothing except a couple of skeletons.

As they were placing the human detritus of war back into the grave, Dennis came over and stopped them. "Listen you blokes, don't say anything to the others but I want to take one of the skulls back, you know for the "Skull Cave"". He hesitated for a moment then continued, "Well we could put it out in front of the tent, it sort of fits in with the "Phantoms of the Jungle".

At this point they looked at each other, each nodding their heads as if they had just agreed to a cup of tea rather than desecrating a VC grave. Then again, the war in Vietnam was like that, the most outrageous suggestions sounded perfectly reasonable in a place where one was walking that fine line between lunacy and insanity. So much so, that sometimes it was the insane ones who were sure that they were just fine and the sane who felt they were crazy.

"Ok Dennis, grab the skull now and we'll finish off the job", said one of the Trackers. With that, Dennis stuffed the skull in his pack while the others threw the last of the dirt over the grave. When they arrived back at the base in Nui Dat, the first thing Dennis did was to place "Charlie" (what else could they have called the skull of a Viet Cong), on a metal pole in front of their tent and called it the "Skull Cave". Charlie would be on display until the Trackers went out on their next operation, when he would be wrapped up and placed in a tin box.

Over the following months, apart from being photographed frequently, Charlie also became a source of black humour. Sometimes beer bottle tops were placed in his eye sockets, or in the evening, there would be a torch or candle inside Charlie's "head". On other occasions "Charlie" became part of the social scene, particularly after someone found a mandibular and wired it up to Charlie's skull. So that whenever they engaged in a drunken sing a long, "Charlie" would be bobbing up and down on the metal pole with his jaw opening and closing in time to the music.

While this may seem callous, it was a progressive thing, a result of the continual exposure to all the things that war brings with it. So the hard, callous behaviour also became a way to deal with or cover the emotional debilitation brought on by this exposure. Black humour was absolutely essential, after all it is not everybody who comes home and says, "It was a hard day at the office, we had to kill two people". Since "Charlie" didn't have a decent burial, at least he became part of a group of people not so different from him, at least in spirit. Every time when they came back from patrol they would place "Charlie" out in front of the "Skull Cave". He became an every day reminder of the ephemeral nature of life and death in war.

Similar to the religious shrine of the Capuchin monks in Rome, who make patterns from the bones and skulls of dead people underneath the church on Piazza Barberini, just so they can meditate on death. Not satisfied with that, the monks do a roaring trade in postcard souvenirs with pictures of the macabre scenes. Soldiers are not alone in this fascination.

Charlie became symbolic of everything that soldiers confront in war. Of course he was even more useful as a reminder of the terminal nature of war. Occasionally one of the section would rub "Charlie" affectionately as they entered the tent saying, "G'Day Charlie, you little bastard, rather you than me mate". After all none of them could look at or touch him without thinking, "No way I'm going to end up like him", particularly if there had been some recent contact, where they had been shot at by some of Charlie's friends. If sometimes there was some kind of vicious joy about all this, it was not because of a premeditated ghoulishness

55

found in psychopaths, but only a normal by-product of war. Those who have never "Done the Business" and wish to criticise should understand that this behaviour was a logical consequence, of the dynamics between two groups of men wishing to remain alive, each at the expense of the other.

There was really only one group that believed that they were fighting for their country; "Charlie" and his friends, since they were already there. While the others were the "invaders" who would only be there for twelve months. Their only aim was to complete their twelve month tour of duty alive and in one piece. In some way this made the sense of euphoria more intense when they survived any contact.

As the months went by, it was obvious that "Charlie" and his friends were winning the war. The "peace talks" were under way in Paris and the movement against the war was growing exponentially. None of the "Phantoms" really wanted to die for a corrupt, non-existent South Vietnamese democracy. What started as a derogatory, black joke, when they opened "The Skull Cave" gradually changed, as the soldiers came to understand their enemy.

An enemy, who could withstand five-hundred-pound bombs, repeated shelling by artillery and mortars, Napalm, chemical defoliants, helicopter gun ships, tanks and, of course, well-rested foreign soldiers who would be there for only twelve months. While Charlie would be there for years, fighting without a break until the end. The only result of that understanding could be respect.

Two days before they were due to go home, late one afternoon as the setting sun intensified the blood red colour of the earth, in-between the lengthening shadows of the rubber trees, some of the "Phantoms of The Jungle" had gathered behind the "Skull Cave".
One of them, Rob, was shovelling dirt from a narrow hole about a metre deep. When he had finished, Dennis handed "Charlie" over to him, wrapped up in a white cloth. He placed "Charlie" gently

into the ground and covered him with the blood red soil, which contrasted eerily with the whiteness of the cloth.

Looking at "Charlie" as he was covered, there was a sense of relief at having completed their tour in one piece. Knowing deep down that there was a lot of luck on their side and that in fact the better side was probably Charlie and his friends. Above all here was a feeling of quiet respect, combined with a deep feeling of guilt at having devalued the dignity of a human life.

That is what war does.

9

A PRISONER OF WAR

*"A prisoner of war is someone who asks you not to kill him
after he has been trying to kill you"*
Winston Churchill

In December of 1969 it was decided to take on the last untouched "secret zone" belonging to Mr Charles in the Nui May Tao mountains. These mountains were on the edge of the Australian area of responsibility and were a VC and NVA stronghold. They had been used for a number of years as a logistic support base providing an administration centre throughout the surrounding provinces. Within this centre, there was thought to be a large hospital complex above and below ground. It should be remembered that by the time the Australians arrived in Vietnam, the Vietnamese had plenty of practice making tunnels during the wars against the Japanese, followed by the French. These systems often had sophisticated networks, in some cases running for hundreds of kilometres with workshops, dormitories, kitchens and hospitals. Where the water table permitted, these systems could be several stories deep with u-bends filled with water to stop the spread of gases and impede the shock waves from explosions.

With this in mind and since specific operations had never been conducted in this area before, everyone could anticipate some serious business. Serious enough for Headquarters to advise the Australian Field Hospital in Vung Tau, to prepare for a higher than normal casualty rate. This piece of information came out years later, after all, there was no need to dampen any enthusiasm.

The helicopter defined the war in Vietnam and the operation in the May Tao was a classic example of this. The Trackers would be inserted in style. Helicopters would be used to place them on top of the mountain range from where they would have an "easy stroll"

59

down. This was much easier than the rifle companies had, of starting at the bottom and working their way up. Unfortunately, when the Trackers reached the bottom, they too had to walk back up the mountain, where they spent Christmas Day with a section from the Mortar Platoon, the only Australians on the mountain.

The actual time spent during the insertion into an LZ was brief, but nonetheless, a tense time for both aircrew and infantrymen. The last few seconds on the approach were the worst. The tension was palpable as the helicopter flared, everyone with their weapons pointed outwards. As soon as the skids touched the ground, everyone poured out of the chopper with the usual desperate 30 or 40 meter sprint and some 50 kilos of gear, more if you carried a radio or the machine gun. The noise of the choppers faded into the distance as they lay on the ground gasping for breath waiting now to see if Charlie had any surprises. Once the LZ was secure, some elements from headquarters flew in and established a more substantial defensive position, while the Trackers secured the outer perimeter that would be their overnight base.

About mid-afternoon, the Trackers were treated to one of the more bizarre incidents of the operation, when a high pitched screeching of bagpipes emanated from the centre of the position. There was the pipe major, who had been specially flown in for the occasion, standing at the summit dressed in a kilt, playing a tune that he had specially composed for the occasion. At the same time two other soldiers were putting up a flagpole, with the Australian and the battalion flag attached to it. Similar to that classic Second World War photo of the marines on Iwo Jima. A symbolic conquering of an enemy. Who knows what Charlie thought about all of this or his opinion of the Australian taste in music. However, with the sun shining, a mug of coffee and some pound cake from an American ration pack, it all took on a festive air, rather than an assault on an enemy bastion. That afternoon was a nice enough way to start an operation.

The following day the Trackers moved out, patrolling down towards the base of the mountain, looking for any sign of Charlie, which came soon enough. On the morning of the third day a couple of bursts fired by the scout of the forward section announced the presence of Mr. Charles, as the cries of "Contact front!" were passed on down the line and the section fanned out into an extended line, with as many weapons as possible facing the area of initial fire.

"Where is he?" yelled the section commander.
"They're still in the fart sack" replied the scout.
"What do you mean; they're still in the fart sack?"
"Just what I said, they're still in their hammocks!" yelled the scout.
"How many are there?" asked the section commander.
"I can see two of them" replied the scout.
At this point there was some laughter as the section commander said, "Are you fucking joking?"
"No", replied the scout, "They look like they're wounded".

Some moments were needed to digest this piece of information. The Trackers thought they had found part of a hospital system but it soon became apparent that the Trackers had stumbled on to a group of wounded VC being carried by a stretcher party to a more secure location. Since there was no return fire it became apparent that these wounded VC had been left behind by their comrades to be taken prisoner. Never-the-less, the Trackers moved cautiously, with one of the sections ready to provide covering fire, the lead section moved slowly towards the two wounded enemy who were both in separate hammocks suspended on a pole. Not as comfortable as the usual stretcher but it worked. As they moved forward, the lead section 2IC, Eric saw another empty hammock with a series of drag marks leading past a number of large rocks. The conclusion was obvious, as he started to follow the track through the rocks.

He could hear others calling out when they had found yet another wounded enemy although these became a distant background noise as he followed the drag marks around the last of the rocks.

Everything was focused on the moment when he would find Charlie. His rifle at the shoulder ready to fire, not knowing what to expect, edging slowly around the corner. Suddenly there was a terrified scream as a young VC sat up two metres in front of him with his hands in the air. Instinctively as he had been trained to do, Eric pulled the trigger twice. This was followed by a deep silence. Both seemed frozen for a few moments. The rifleman needed time to process the fact that for some inexplicable reason, from the start, he had left the rifle safety catch locked on safe, while the VC processed the fact that he was still alive. The rifleman lowered his weapon as the VC lowered his hands. Both of them were trembling, full of adrenaline and fear. At that moment the section commander came around the corner,

"So you've got one too, they're all over the place", he said.

"Mmm, yeah", replied the Eric with a shaky voice.

"What's the matter with you?" asked the section commander, "You look like you've seen a ghost".

"Umm, well nothing, just feeling a bit tired", said Eric.

"OK, you stay here and I'll get the medic to have a look at this one when he's finished with the others", said the section commander, as he walked back along the track.

Then Eric saw for the first time, that the VC had been wounded in the right thigh, which was full of gangrene, infested with maggots. He lit a cigarette with still trembling hands. "Christ, the poor bastard is really fucked", he thought to himself. Then the VC put his hand to his mouth indicating he would like a cigarette. Eric lit another and gave it to him shaking his head, "This is fucking stupid, totally fucking stupid, one minute we're trying to kill each other, the next we're sharing cigarettes", he thought to himself.

They waited for nearly half an hour while the medic treated the other VC preparing them to be medivaced by helicopter. During which time Eric shared his cigarettes with his recent enemy.
Occasionally they would look at each other, with the awkwardness of two young men confronting each other over the vast gulf of a totally different propaganda, culture and language.

The only thing they had in common was a war and an unlikely combination of circumstances that allowed a badly wounded Vietnamese to live and share the cigarettes of a young Australian who would have killed him but for his own forgetfulness. The Australian was doubly lucky. He had avoided a lifetime of regret by not killing a badly wounded and unarmed Vietnamese. When the medic arrived he looked as if he hadn't slept for a week.

"Jesus you look fucked", said the Eric.
Yeah, well, I've had to clean up four really fucked up Nogs", replied the medic.
"You mean we've taken five POWs?" asked the Eric.
"There are three more after this bloke, so we've got eight", replied the medic.
"Shit! There's only twenty seven of us, I hope there are no more", said Eric.

The medic started working on the VC, "Christ! This bloke is a real mess, his leg is moving by itself", he said referring to the maggots in the upper thigh of the Vietnamese. Then the medic started working on the nauseating task of cleaning up the wounded Vietnamese. Eric turned away, unable to tolerate the stench or watch, as the medic swabbed away the rotting flesh before applying a bandage, while the young Vietnamese would make a hissing sound when the pain was too much to bear.

"These are tough bastards", thought Eric, as he smoked what must have been his fifth cigarette.

"Right", said the medic, after ten minutes, "This one is right to go, do you want to give us a hand to carry him up to the chopper pad?"

"Yeah, no problem", replied Eric.

"OK, I've got three more to look at, so I'll get one of the others to come down and you can bring him up", said the Medic as he left to attend to the next POW.

The Vietnamese was covered in sweat and breathing heavily as he dealt with the residual pain of having a good portion of his right thigh excavated. As the prisoner's pain subsided, Eric opened his nearly empty water bottle and gave it to the Vietnamese, who drained the contents and gave it back to him with a weak smile in thanks. After a short while one of the riflemen arrived with a pole and hammock to carry the prisoner up to the helicopter pad.

"You right to go?" asked the rifleman.

"Yea, let's load him up", replied Eric.

They placed the VC on the hammock then gently lifted the pole onto their shoulders and started to carry him up to the helicopter pad, accompanied by the VC's almost continuous hissing sound. They bumped and swayed for twenty exhausting minutes over the rocks up a steep incline to the top of the ridge where a large flat rock served as the helicopter landing pad.

They laid the VC on the ground and waited for the medivac to arrive. The other POWs were some distance away being carried up to the makeshift LZ, which had just enough room for a medivac helicopter provided it stayed with only one skid on the rock and the other skid airborne. This would require some skilful flying as the pilot would have to compensate by staying somewhere between hovering and landing as the POWs were loaded onto the helicopter. This was difficult enough under normal flying conditions, let alone when the distinct possibility of being shot at was put into the equation followed by the usual overloaded takeoff. Flying inside the envelope on operations in Vietnam was an option generally available, only when flying empty.

The three of them sat smoking a cigarette until the rifleman broke the silence.

"So what do you reckon happens to these Nogs when they are taken back?" he asked Eric.

"Apparently after the hospital fixes them up, they get handed over to the South Vietnamese and they deal with them". He replied with sideways glance at their prisoner, who stared unflinchingly back as if he knew exactly what the discussion was about.

"That means a serious bit of interrogation", the rifleman said, "I mean the VN's are all the same for this sort of shit, aren't they" he said more as a statement than a question. In that moment Eric realized that the POW knew exactly what the future held, his demeanour being a way to cover his fear of how this would end. There was a long silence as the three of them reflected on the inevitable conclusion for the POW. The South Vietnamese Army was renowned for torturing prisoners, as was the North.

The sound of the approaching helicopter broke the silence, as the two Australians looked at the POW with a sense of guilt, for being participants in a shameful charade. While the helicopter hovered with one skid on the rock, they picked up the POW and moved towards the helicopter. Eric placed his packet of cigarettes into the shirt pocket of the POW, who gave him a weak smile.

As they slid the prisoner into the helicopter, he raised his head and yelled something into Eric's ear over the noise of the helicopter, who nodded his head, stepping back from the helicopter as it powered up for take off. The prisoner and the 2IC looked directly at each other for a long moment. Both of them knowing, that the VC would not have long to live once he was in the hands of the South Vietnamese interrogators. In that moment there was a sudden understanding that in other circumstances they could have

65

been friends. Just as suddenly the helicopter fell away from the ridge line.

With the sound of the helicopter fading into the distance Eric turned to one of the riflemen who spoke some Vietnamese and asked, "So what does *kam ern* mean in Vietnamese"?

"I think it means thank you, why?" replied the rifleman.

"Oh, nothing important, just wondering that's all".

Years later, Eric realised that the young Vietnamese was one of the bravest men he had ever met.

AFTERWORD

In December 1969, the Tracker platoon encountered a large group of North Vietnamese carrying eight wounded. As soon as the contact was initiated, the North Vietnamese wounded were left behind, with the hope that they would be taken as prisoners of war. In spite of the fact that just days previously, two Australians had been killed and five wounded in the next valley, all of these wounded prisoners were treated no differently to Australian wounded. Their wounds were treated, they were given food, water and cigarettes. This was probably because all front line soldiers have to deal with the same physical discomforts, friend and foe alike. In these physical extremes it is better to treat the enemy well. After all one day the situation could be reversed, reinforced with the knowledge that those who don't show mercy cannot expect to receive it.

10

Trajan

"Asking Charlie about the dogs, would have been
like asking a lamp post the same question" Anon.

Jet arrived into the world during February of 1965. He was born
in a small town in the Blue Mountains to the west of Sydney.
A Labrador – Kelpie cross, he was the smallest of the litter.
Perhaps that was why the old lady, on hearing of the Army tracker
dog programme decided to offer Jet as a candidate.

The Army sourced most of their tracker dogs from the pound
and occasionally from private owners. The majority of the dogs
were Labrador or Labrador cross breeds, since these had the right
combination of physical resilience, a good "nose" and placid
demeanour. Unlike the so-called "War Dogs" of the Doberman or
Alsatian variety which were generally too highly strung and
normally only used as guard dogs. Although, the Americans did
use them occasionally as "Attack Dogs" against Charlie, without
much success. After all, a set of dogs teeth is hardly a match
against a Kalashnikov rifle.

The tracker dogs needed a very different demeanour with an
ability to track a scent several hours old, sometimes for
consecutive days. At the end of which, more often than not, there
would be a cacophony of rifle fire and sometimes explosions of
grenades, mortars and / or artillery. This carried with it the risk of
being wounded or killed. Obviously the dogs wouldn't understand
that particular downside of this work. For the successful
candidates it was a great game to play with a very noisy finish.

The dogs that were selected would also have to cope with
airborne insertions and extractions by helicopters, which included
being winched up through the jungle canopy about thirty or forty
metres above the ground, as well as insertions by armoured
personnel carriers. Although they weren't formally trained for it,

there were occasions, when they detected mines or booby traps. While learning that skill as "OJT" (On the Job Training) was no problem for the dog, anyone in the vicinity was less than enthusiastic. In some way, the tracker dogs were the special forces of the dog world.

After a series of tests and medical checks, Jet was found to be a suitable candidate for the initial phase of training and following usual army procedure, was given his army number (D7NI7). Since all army tracker dogs were named after Roman emperors, his "civilian name" was changed and from that moment on he was called Trajan.

The anglicised name of the Roman emperor Traiano, who was actually called Traiano Optimus or Trajan the Best (because he was regarded as one of the best emperors that ruled the Roman Empire).

While it seems a little unfair that a dog could be conscripted into the Army without even a whimper, we should remember that this was the late sixties and a few thousand young Australians were being conscripted every year for service in Vietnam. So the dogs were treated on an equal footing with humans and sometimes vice- versa.

Some months prior to Trajan's enlistment, Russell McDonald had volunteered for the Australian Army. Having completed his basic training and Infantry training he was posted to the Combat Tracking Centre, where he was trained as a dog handler. This was a highly specialised type of work, with a risk component not much below a Kamikaze pilot, for both the dog and the handler, particularly since the tracking team would be used when the enemy presence was already established. Effectively when the team was called out, a fire fight with Charlie was a near certainty.

In the months that followed Russell or "Mooka" as everyone called him, would train several different dogs in various phases of their training, which gave him exposure to the different personalities that exist in the dog world. Some were a bit too aggressive or lazy, some just wanted to play, and they all had their strengths and weaknesses.

The first dog that Mooka had to train from scratch was "Virgil", who initially seemed ideal for the work. He was good in the discipline phase, very obedient and a better-than-average tracker. All was perfect until the next phase which involved the use of blank ammunition. Virgil had been following the track for about twenty minutes when he stopped to point. Mooka pulled him back with the lead and ran his hand along his back saying, "Good boy, good boy". At that moment the soldier playing the part of the enemy fired a shot. Virgil took a huge leap out of Mooka's arms and ran in the opposite direction. He was so fast that Mooka had no time to react as he watched the last two metres of the tracking lead snaking through the scrub. With that reaction, obviously Virgil was a highly intelligent dog. After all, what do you do if someone is trying to shoot you? It is not unreasonable to leave as quickly as possible.

Unfortunately in the army, running away is not an acceptable response. In fact, they require everyone to run towards the danger and have the legs override the brain's instructions to run in the opposite direction. Clearly Virgil would be totally useless as a hunter of Viet Cong. It took a couple of hours to find Virgil, hiding in the low scrub and two days later Virgil was discharged from the army with what was known as a "SNARLER" or "Services no longer in the interest of the army". The same category as a conscientious objector. He was a nice dog.

At this point, after being involved with the training of several dogs, most of which had been very average, Mooka had decided there was probably no such animal as the perfect tracker dog. About a week later Mooka was called up to the Orderly Room to be told by the Sergeant Major that next morning a new dog would be arriving for evaluation and was given the dog's file.

Name: TRAJAN   Number: D7N17

"Well sir, I hope this one turns out better, I seem to be getting all the duds" said Mooka.
"Don't worry. Half of them never make the grade. Let me know what you think in a week", replied the sergeant major.
Next morning Mooka woke up with a sense of expectation, "New day, new dog, who knows?" he thought to himself, "This one has to be better than the last few".
As he approached the kennels he saw the clerk with the paperwork on a clipboard in one hand and the lead in the other hand with the new dog sitting quietly beside him.
"Right Mooka, this is the new one, just sign here for him", said the clerk in flat bored tone. He had done this many times.
Mooka took the clipboard and glanced at the form, "So, this is Trajan, he doesn't look too bad, pretty quiet", said Mooka.
"Yeah, well if he goes ok, you'll have him from start to finish" said the clerk as he walked away.
Mooka looked down at the dog, "So Trajan, what do you know?"
"Let's try a couple of things", he said stepping back a few metres.
"Trajan, come here boy, come on", he called motioning at the same time with his hand. Trajan moved his head to one side and started to walk slowly towards Mooka, stopping beside his leg.
"Good boy, good boy", said Mooka as he rubbed the dog's flank.
"Ok, now sit, sit", he commanded as Trajan looked up at him quizzically. Once again with his head to one side, with a direct stare that seemed to say "I'm trying to understand, what do you want me to do?" That direct look with his head to one side would become a characteristic of Trajan's personality.
"We have some work to do Trajan, so we may as well start now", said Mooka.

70

That first day together was focused on the basic obedience commands of sit, come here, down and stay. By late afternoon, both Trajan and Mooka had done four hours of intensive training, which was a lot for a young dog of twenty months and a young soldier of 18 years. When Trajan went back to his kennel, Mooka gave him his food with a raw egg to condition his coat and some calcium for his bones. As Trajan was eating, Mooka realised that Trajan ate quite slowly. There was an air of calmness about the dog in everything he did, which made him different from the others. Even when Mooka scolded him during the discipline training, the dog never flinched or lowered his head, he just looked directly at him with his head to one side.

"Well, not bad for day one, I hope he goes on like this", thought Mooka.

The next day started with what would become the standard routine for both of them; breakfast followed by some light grooming, checking the dog's mouth, teeth, footpads and nails.

Grooming and checking was done at the beginning and end of each day, not for appearances but for practical reasons. Since the dogs were out in the bush training, there was always the possibility of thorns or rocks cutting their pads or picking up ticks, both which could lead to serious infections. After the grooming they started again on the basic obedience training followed by some short walks with a tracking harness that was fixed around the dog's chest with a long seven metre lead, which Trajan adapted to from the start.

Then came Trajan's first real training as a tracker dog; his first short track. It was done by having Mooka disappear into the bush about one hundred and fifty metres away, while another handler would have Trajan in harness on the long tracking lead. Since Trajan knew Mooka's scent the short track would be relatively easy. All of the handlers were trained as visual trackers, so the second handler with the dog would know what to look for and encourage the dog on the track with the command "seekem,

seekem". Once this was accomplished several times, Trajan was rewarded with a "good boy hug", a pat and the occasional dog biscuit.

After several days they progressed to longer more realistic tracks with up to as many as four soldiers laying the track while Mooka would urge the dog on, "seekem Trajan, seekem". For Trajan this was such a good game, following the scent of the track and finding the soldiers at the end of it.

His next test would be crucial so that he could learn to "point" from a distance. When he was within one hundred metres of the soldiers at the end of the track, they would fire a shot. The idea being that the dog would associate the gunshot with the strength of the scent and know when to stop or "point".

Every dog points in slightly different ways and not always in the classic way, with the paw raised and the nose and tail extended. Trajan would simply stop with a front paw off the ground and his ears forward. He understood the game very quickly and never had any problem with the sound of rifle fire. He was soon pointing from one hundred to one hundred and fifty metres away. As the weeks went past they progressed to longer, older and more difficult tracks of one kilometre long and six hours old. Then they concentrated on speed. The necessity to move quickly without loosing the track was crucial. Charlie would be moving as quickly as possible and if the track was lost then valuable time was lost finding the track again, which would allow Charlie to apply the guerrilla's motto;

"He who fights and runs away, lives to fight another day".

Both Trajan and Mooka worked in harmony, the days and weeks blending into one another until they found themselves doing multi-day tracks. Mooka carrying food and water for both of them, so both would be equally thirsty and hungry. They slept together on the ground, rising just before the sun, following tracks all-day; short and long ones. Occasionally they would track scent over water when the track crossed streams, it was possible to do this with recent tracks, no breeze and a good dog.

Sometimes the going was really steep which was harder for Mooka; while he was carrying at least forty kilos, one hand held the lead and the other his rifle. Added to this, at the same time Mooka had to try and confirm the track using his visual tracking skills and keep a lookout for the soldiers playing the part of the "Enemy". Training for war did not allow for tiredness or lack of concentration, for either the dog or the handler.

Almost instinctively Trajan knew when Mooka was feeling the pace, probably because he felt the pressure on the tracking lead. Whatever the reason, Trajan would turn his head, look at Mooka and slow down, making it easier for Mooka to follow the track.

Every couple of hours, if they hadn't crossed any creeks, Mooka would pull out the water bottle and they would both have a drink. Food was at morning and night and if there was lunch, it was a couple of biscuits for Trajan.

After months of training they were fit, toughened up, used to the discomfort of living in the bush, they were ready for their final test; a three day old track of one and a half kilometres. This they completed in one of the fastest times registered at the Combat Tracking Centre. Finally they were a team.

By April of 1968 there was a requirement for another dog and handler in Vietnam. While Trajan was next on the list, trained and ready there was a problem; Mooka was under 19 and too young to be sent on active service. So it was arranged for Trajan to be sent with another handler. When Mooka was told that Trajan would be going without him he was quite upset. The normal procedure was that the dog and handler went together on their first posting and Mooka expected that he would be sent to Vietnam when he was nineteen, with Trajan; it was not to be.

Two days later, Trajan's ears pricked up as he saw Mooka approaching, he started to walk towards the end of the run in anticipation of the games they would play. Chasing after other soldiers, finding them, followed by Trajan's favourite crunchy biscuits. Then Trajan saw that Mooka did not have the tracking harness with the long lead that they used to play their games.

Mooka looked at Trajan, ran his hand along his flank saying, "Well boy, you're going and I'm not". Trajan looked at him with his head to one side knowing that Mooka was not happy. He sniffed the back of Mooka's hand and licked it, as if to comfort him.

As the vehicle stopped in front of the kennels, Mooka straightened, gave Trajan a rub behind the ear and said, "Good luck mate, you taught me a lot". Then turned around and walked towards the vehicle saying to the driver, "You can pick up all the paperwork and Trajan's gear at the orderly room".
"You don't want to come with us for the ride?" asked the driver.
"Not really, thanks mate", replied Mooka.

The driver placed Trajan in the back of the vehicle and drove off as Mooka walked away and Trajan watched him with his head cocked to one side as he always did when he was trying to understand. He watched Mooka, until they turned a corner and he disappeared from view.

Eleven days after Trajan left the Combat tracking Centre, Mooka and his new dog Tago, were posted to 6 Battalion in Townsville. With Mooka was a second team, Willie and Titus; they would be the nucleus of two complete combat tracking teams within the battalion's Tracker Platoon.

Each team consisted of a tracker dog and handler with a light automatic weapon, a cover-man who carried a machine gun to provide maximum fire power for the protection of the dog and handler, followed by the team commander, signaller, and two or three riflemen, most of whom were qualified visual trackers.

Besides their main role of following and tracking down Charlie, from intelligence information or after fire fights with other platoons, the Tracker Platoon provided two other functions; as a logical flow on from their observational skills they were used as reconnaissance teams. Well forward of the battalion to gather intelligence and for setting day and night ambush patrols. The second extra function, since it originally functioned as the Anti-Tank Platoon, was the provision of protection for the battalion FSB on operations, using Anti-Tank weapons. These extra requirements meant that everybody was cross-trained in all facets of the platoon's work with the exception of the dogs and their handlers whose role was highly specialised.

Mooka's new dog Tago was good enough as a tracker dog, until he developed the disconcerting habit of chasing any rabbits or kangaroos that crossed the track. In spite of Tago's idiosyncratic behaviour, the two dogs and their handlers were soon integrated within the platoon, doing similar training as before but with a complete combat tracking team of six to eight soldiers.

Two of the teams would work with the handlers and their dogs, as the other two teams trained on recce patrols or with the anti-tank weapons, alternating with each other over the weeks and months until they could work together, almost instinctively.

While Mooka and the Trackers were going through their gruelling training schedule in the Queensland rainforests, Trajan had to adapt to a very different situation in Vietnam. Apart from the pungent scents and foetid atmosphere, there was the almost continuous noise of artillery and mortars and while his new handler Nigel was good, Trajan missed the discreet reserve of Mooka. Then there were the times when the noise was really loud and there would be this continuous cracking sound overhead. Although Trajan had heard this before in Australia on exercises, it was never as intense or as often. The atmosphere amongst the soldiers was tense, not the same as back in Australia, where it was much more relaxed.

Of course this time the game was the real thing and that cracking sound was the sound made by live bullets fired by Charlie. Whenever the cracking sounds started, Trajan could sense something in the atmosphere that he had never known before, the fear that emanated from the soldiers. Sometimes he could almost taste it and when that happened, the game wasn't so much fun.

Meanwhile back in Australia Mooka and the rest of the Trackers were undergoing a gruelling training schedule to prepare them for Vietnam. The months passed quickly, the training was nearly complete. There was a three week course at the Jungle Warfare Centre to be completed followed by ten days pre-embarkation leave before the Trackers would leave for Vietnam.
Shortly before the Trackers were due to leave, while they were on a tracking exercise with the dogs North of Townsville, Titus was bitten by a snake and died shortly afterwards.

After nearly a year, Titus had become part of the platoon and he was not "Just another dog". For a while there was a cloud over the Trackers and some time was needed for the Trackers to regain their exuberance. By the time they were due to leave, everyone was aware that Tago would not be going to Vietnam. Aside from his penchant for chasing wildlife when he was on track, he was the only Golden Labrador amongst the other tracker dogs and a Golden Labrador moving through the jungles of Vietnam would be rather obvious. This was to be a blonde free zone.

Tago would never know it, but his lack of concentration and colour would result in him being posted to Malaysia, a holiday camp, just down the road from a serious war. The loss of Titus and the fact that Tago was not going to Vietnam, meant that the Trackers would be using dogs already in country, and Mooka was elated to know that when he arrived in Vietnam, Trajan would be his dog again.

After nearly a year in Vietnam, Trajan had a regular cadence in his life; three or four weeks on operations when they would play the sometimes noisy "tracking games" followed by three or four days of rest. Suddenly the cadence changed and the rest period was much longer than usual. They had been at the Australian base in Nui Dat for nearly ten days when Nigel came walking up to the kennels. He opened the gate and stood in front of Trajan, bent down and gave Trajan a "good boy" hug, as if he had just completed a successful track.

"Well boy", he said, "I'm going to miss you but you're going to have a nice surprise today".

The Australian Army had less than twenty dog handlers; theirs was a small world and Nigel knew that Mooka had been Trajan's original trainer. Obviously Mooka would be Trajan's next handler. At that moment a number of the other soldiers came up to Trajan and gave him a pat or a hug.

"We better get going, the new handler should be at the orderly room by now", said one of them
"Yeah, right", said Nigel, "I'll go and pick him up".

Nigel knew that Mooka would be impatient to see Trajan again.
For Trajan the atmosphere must have been quite difficult to comprehend. There was no tension, no sense of urgency that was usual after they had rested and were preparing for another operation. At the same time Trajan could sense that Nigel was not happy. It was all very confusing. Of course Trajan could not know that it was all over, they had completed their tour in Vietnam and everyone was going home. Except Trajan.
Nigel showed Mooka his new "home", in a row of tents where the rest of the platoon would be housed when they arrived. They then proceeded in the direction of the Kennels, stopping about fifty metres away.

"Look Mooka, why don't you go up to Trajan on your own? I mean he's yours now and well, I've already said my goodbye", he finished the sentence awkwardly.

"Yeah ok", said Mooka, understanding exactly how Nigel felt.
The handlers always developed strong connections with their dogs, all the more so on active service.
"Maybe see ya back in OZ", said Nigel as they shook hands.
"Yea maybe", replied Mooka as he started towards the kennels, with anticipation.

Trajan saw Mooka coming towards him, but it wasn't until he picked up that familiar scent on the light breeze, that Trajan wagged his tail in recognition. He never jumped around much, like Mooka he was always a bit reserved.
"Good boy, you remember, yea you remember, well done!" Said Mooka leaning over to give Trajan a hug as Trajan licked the back of his hand. Two mates were back together again.

A few days later, the rest of the Trackers arrived in Nui Dat. Almost immediately they were sent out on a series of short two or three day tactical patrols in the quiet areas of the province. This was designed to familiarise them with the operational environment. There were no contacts with Charlie, although a few old tracks were seen, there was nothing of interest; just lots of walking with heavy loads. If they felt tired, it was nothing to the exhaustion they would feel on the long operations to follow.

Their first serious operation was to be to the North of their base in Nui Dat, where Charlie had been quite active. Briefings were held, equipment checked and double-checked. Rations issued along with ammunition. Something for life, something for death.
War can be quite even handed.
Early in the morning the tracker teams boarded the APCs (Armoured Personnel Carriers), Mooka and Trajan sat on top of the carrier with one of the tracker teams as they headed off. Trajan with his head up and mouth open in what looked like a huge smile, enjoyed the wind as it swept his ears back while they sped through the villages towards the fire support base from which they would be operating for the next month.

Shortly after their arrival, the Trackers established themselves on the outer perimeter of the base. Their U shaped weapon pits were dug for two men and covered with sandbags; the two vertical tails of the U would be their "room" for the next month.

The Trackers adapted quickly to the operational routine of the Fire Support Base. The early morning and evening stand to, in which everyone was ready, at the most likely time that Charlie would choose to attack. This would be followed by clearing patrols at the same time of day, to check for enemy movement.

In between all of this, there were night ambush patrols and daily fighting and or recce patrols, most of which resulted in exhausted boredom. It was some time before Mooka and Trajan were called on to play their part.

One afternoon, about halfway through the operation they were part of a fighting patrol, when one of the visual trackers spotted some ground sign and small shrubs, which had been pushed over by what appeared to be "Ho Chi Minh" sandals. These were sandals made from car tyres and the footwear of choice amongst the VC. Not that there was much choice. The patrol changed order so that the scout/visual tracker went to the rear as Mooka and Trajan would follow the track with a cover man/machine gunner behind them, followed by the section commander and the riflemen. Trajan was wagging his tail in anticipation as Mooka clipped on the tracking lead.

"We're doing this for real now", said Mooka as he let out some slack on the twenty foot lead.
"Ok, seekem! Seekem boy!"

Trajan was off. His head up as he "air sniffed", a sign that the trail was fresh since he didn't need to sniff close to the ground. As they moved forward Mooka was sweeping the ground in front of him, his weapon following his eyes. From right to left, the opposite of reading, a method to slow down the process and be more thorough in his search for Charlie. At the same time he was watching for any sign of a point from Trajan. The tension was building as the focus narrowed as they arrived at the edge of a creek.

Mooka was in his own world of total concentration; right to left, check the dog; right to left, check the dog, right to left check - - shit! He's pointing! They both stopped dead still. Trajan with his paw slightly raised his ears forward, not moving. Mooka went down on one knee, his heart pounding as he crouched down, searching the jungle intensely. He saw the water in the creek had been muddied, leading up to the tracks on the other side.
Charlie was close, very close. Everyone else was frozen still, watching, listening and waiting.

After a couple of minutes the patrol commander gave the hand signal to keep tracking. A second point would mean Charlie could be as close as thirty metres away. The tension was palpable, as the patrol slowly moved forward.

Mooka's concentration was so intense, rivulets of sweat trickled down the back of his neck, unnoticed, along with a large black mosquito sucking on the side of his face. Trajan felt the lead tighten as Mooka slowed him down. By now the patrol was taking seconds between each step. High stepping; balancing on one foot at a time to avoid the undergrowth. Then placing the foot down rolling it from the outside inwards to avoid making any noise. If Charlie saw this it would seem like a line of men doing a chorus line act; in slow motion.

Then came a silence that is probably only found in the premonition of death in war, more specifically in the jungle, where the visual distance is rarely more than twenty metres.

Trajan stopped and pointed again.

Suddenly there were two short bursts of machinegun fire from the cover-man. Instantly Mooka dropped to the ground, pulling Trajan back behind him, protecting him, while he looked for Charlie.

"Contact Front!" yelled Bill, the cover man.

Immediately everyone else repeated the two words to the one behind, so that they were all aware and knew that they would move into a contact drill.

"I think I got him", said Bill.
"Where is he?" replied Mooka.
"About 15 metres to your right, I think he came up from the creek".
"Right, we'll wait until they sweep through", said Mooka. As he pulled out his water bottle and gave Trajan a drink before taking a long mouthful himself, at the same time keeping a watchful eye to his front. The adrenaline was still pumping.

"Good boy, well done!" he said to Trajan rubbing the dog's flank. Trajan looked pleased with himself, wagging his tail, panting, with his tongue slobbering over Mooka's hand. From Trajan's point of view another successful "game" was completed.

After the area to their front had been cleared, they moved forward, walking past one very dead Viet Cong. The machine gun had taken off the top of his skull with surgical precision, allowing his brains to spill out onto the ground, as he lay in the contorted way of people killed by high velocity gunfire. He was young, perhaps eighteen and as the patrol walked past him there was no sense of victory. For the newly baptised, a sense of horrific wonder, for the old hands who had seen it before, there could only be detachment.

That afternoon as they set up their defensive position for the night, most of the team came up with lots of "good boy" pats for Trajan and if the atmosphere was a bit tense, it was in some way relieved by the presence of Trajan. It would become almost a form of therapy after a contact with Charlie. When things could seem rather heavy, instinctively, they would talk to a dog. Trajan and the other dogs became touchstones of humanity in circumstances that were inhuman. One could talk to them; of course they could not answer back. Freud and Pavlov rolled into one.

Now the tempo of war was picking up and not long after they returned to their FSB, Trajan and Mooka were sent out to one of the rifle companies as a mini team at the request of a platoon to follow up a wounded VC. A small Bell Helicopter was sent to pick them up. This was a two seater with just enough room for Trajan. Helicopters were his favourite ride and flying in the Bell was like sitting in a plexiglass bubble, as they skimmed over the tree tops.

As they neared the LZ, Mooka listened to the pilot as he requested identification with a smoke grenade, to avoid the possibility of an ambush by Mr. Charles.

"Four One this is Possum Two Zero, throw smoke over".

"This is Four One, smoke thrown over"

"This is Possum Two Zero, I see yellow over"

"This is Four One, yellow thrown over"

"Possum Two Zero roger out"

The Pilot looked at Mooka, "We're going in, are you two ready?"

Mooka nodded, he could see some of the platoon on the edge of the clearing.

"Good Luck", said the pilot, as the Bell made a steep turn into a small clearing, and then flared as it settled onto the ground. Trajan leapt out with Mooka right behind him, the Bell rising away almost at the same time as Mooka's feet touched the ground. Within seconds they were absorbed into the dense jungle.

The platoon commander gave Mooka a quick briefing, indicating that one or more wounded VC was up ahead. Working with a normal infantry platoon was very different from the tracker

82

team. There was no trained visual tracker or cover-man, making this a much more risky situation for both of them.

Trajan and Mooka moved to the front of the lead section, taking over from the forward scout, with the machine gunner behind them. Mooka picked up the blood trail, which consisted of the occasional drops of blood every few metres and clipped the long tracking lead to the harness.

"Ok boy, seekem, seekem", he said.

Trajan pulled eagerly on the lead. This was easy, no doubt about the scent. They had covered about a thousand metres when Trajan started to slow up. Suddenly Trajan pointed, his paw raised and ears forward. Mooka felt that by now familiar feeling of adrenaline. He signalled for the platoon commander to come up and told him that Charlie was about one hundred metres away. The platoon commander seemed sceptical and ordered Mooka and Trajan to continue. Now they were back in that zone of premonition, the zone between life and death. Total concentration by both man and dog as the trail started to curve sharply to the right, which if they kept on, would put them as potential recipients of friendly fire. Then Trajan pointed again.

At that moment Mooka picked up some movement with his peripheral vision. It was the section commander about eighty metres away when he should have been ten metres away. He was signalling one thumb down which meant enemy.

Mooka dropped like a stone, pulling Trajan back.

Suddenly there was an eruption of rifle and machine gun fire, which continued for about a minute.

"The idiots! Bloody bastards", he said to himself, at the same time pushing Trajan behind him.

"Steady boy, steady", he whispered to Trajan, while he searched for Charlie.

When the lead section finally caught up with Mooka, they were rather embarrassed. No words were exchanged. Charlie was still out there. As the rifle platoon moved forward, they had an interpreter call out to the VC, telling him to surrender. Eventually, a rather sorry looking VC hands in the air, leaning against a tree, stood up on one leg. He was standing on one leg because the other leg was missing the front part of the foot. Above the remains of the foot was a crude tourniquet.

The area was cleared to ensure that Charlie had no friends nearby. While a helicopter medivac was called for the prisoner. A medic applied a fresh tourniquet and gave him some water and a cigarette. Throughout all this the VC never said a word. Just a short hissing sound when there was pain. This type of stoic courage was a hallmark of the VC, which quickly gained them a lot of respect.

As they waited for Possum to come and pick up Trajan and Mooka, there were congratulatory pats for Trajan.
"These dogs really work, I knew that they were pretty good", said the section commander.
"Is that right", replied Mooka. "So how come you dropped right back after the first point?"
"Well, umm". The section commander was extremely embarrassed.
"Well nothing, you left me out like a shag on a rock", said Mooka.

A long silence followed finally broken by the sound of the approaching helicopter. The identifying marker from the smoke grenade swirled through the rotor blades, as they both jumped aboard. Trajan happy in the helicopter, as it moved off, banking steeply away from the clearing.

"How was it?" asked the pilot
"It wasn't very interesting" replied Mooka as Trajan looked up at him his head to one side, as usual.

84

For the next ten months the dogs of Tracker Platoon, Trajan, Marcus and Milo would sniff their way through the jungles of Phuoc Tuy province. Through the wet season when everything was soaked and the dry season when everyone was continually dehydrated, the tracker dogs and their handlers were always there, providing a unique and reliable early warning system.

On their birthday, the dogs were given a can of beer while the handlers had many more. When the Trackers went on leave, so did the dogs. On one occasion when Mooka was on a five-day leave pass, one of the Trackers was given the task of looking after Trajan. He let him out of his kennel for a walk and Trajan disappeared for two days. No one knows where he was during that time; probably like most on those leave passes he "found a girlfriend"

Trajan met ministers of state, military generals even the Prime Minister of Australia when he came to visit the troops. Invariably all of them went to meet the tracker dogs.

Of course at the end there was the bitter-sweet goodbye. The day when the handlers would walk up to say their last goodbye. For Mooka it was particularly difficult. Together they had completed fourteen tracks. That was fourteen times they had protected each other. He took all of Trajan's gear to the orderly room then walked up to the kennels and opened up Trajan's run.

"Well mate, this time it really is goodbye", said Mooka as Trajan looked up at him his head to one side, trying to understand while Mooka held him for a moment.

"C'mon fella better get back in", said Mooka as he closed the gate. He turned around and walked away through one of the many small clouds of dust that came with dry season, wiping his eyes as he walked past the orderly room.

"You okay?" asked the orderly room corporal.

"Yeah, just this bloody dust gets in your eyes", he lied.

Trajan watched him walk away until he disappeared amongst the rubber trees.

AFTER WORD

The "Combat Tracking School" was a development born out of the "Police Action" carried out against the Communists in what was then Malaya where tracker dogs were first used by the British with occasional Australian involvement.

Since this period in Malaya was experimental, these efforts were sometimes quite naïve and clumsy. The choice of breeds selected, included Dobermans and German Shepherds. These were good guard dogs but tended to be highly strung, with a low tolerance for sudden loud noises like grenades and gunshots. Not a good look for a war dog. The last thing a dog handler wants is his dog losing the plot in the middle of a fire-fight.

When the Australian Army established the Combat Tracking School at Ingleburn, just south of Sydney in the mid sixties' the Labrador was considered to be the most suitable breed. Preferably the Kelpie cross variety, which was more adaptable to the harsh conditions of jungle warfare.

After three years of continuous operational service, the dogs were given as pets to civilians or diplomatic staff living in Saigon, with the exception of Cassius who died of heat exhaustion.

Between 1967 and 1971 eleven tracker dogs were sent to Vietnam. None came home. Of the eleven tracker dogs, only one remains unaccounted for; that exceptional dog, Trajan.

Between 1969 and 1970, during their tour of duty, 6RAR/NZ (ANZAC) Battalion had twenty four soldiers killed in action and one hundred and forty eight wounded in action. Of those, not a single casualty was sustained by the Tracker Platoon. A testament not only to good leadership and some good luck, but also to Trajan and the other dogs like him, who were responsible for avoiding many more Australian casualties.

Today there are four memorials dotted around Australia to these "Dogs of War", as they were affectionately called. From the West coast in Perth to the East coast in Brisbane, as well as the South Australian coastal town of Goolwa, where, etched in granite, are the eleven names of these "Dogs of War".

Beside the names, fittingly, is an etching of a photo taken in Vietnam showing Trajan with his head to one side, looking directly at Mooka, ready to leave for another game together. The last is a simple one in Hobart consisting of a walk, with paving stones on which are inscribed a dedication to the dogs in general, but with one in particular: "Trajan – A Mate Left Behind".

Goolwa Memorial SA

AUSTRALIAN WAR DOGS
THAT SERVED IN VIETNAM
1967 - 1971

CEASAR

CASSIUS

JANUS

JULIAN

JUNO

JUSTIN

MARCIAN

MARCUS

MILO

TIBER

TRAJAN

11

RIVERS OF BURNING ICE

"My health was menaced, terror came for days.
I slept, because when I was wake, I was ripe for death"
Rimbaud. "A Season of Hell"

Everything seemed irritating that morning, exacerbated by the headache, which woke him up, at least an hour before dawn. In half an hour the platoon would be awake for "Stand To". This was the time of day when Charlie was most likely to attack, hoping to catch the Trackers off guard.

Since he was awake, David started the morning routine of packing his gear, while he waited for the commencement of "Stand To". Every movement was an effort requiring the utmost concentration for the simplest task. He couldn't be alert, even when the platoon was at "Stand To", for an hour around first light. Just keeping his eyes open was an effort in between the shivering tremors brought about by the freezing cold that enveloped him every few minutes. All of this, combined with a feeling of unexplainable anxiety, left him barely able to move let alone function. It was not the anxiety of an imminent contact with "Charlie". No, it was the anxiety of something horribly wrong within, borne from the weakness, which overcame him every few minutes.

"Maybe it's the flu" he thought to himself, "What a fucked up place this is, the middle of summer and I'm freezing".

A couple of hours later the platoon started to continue their patrol with the section 2IC moving like a zombie, following the machine gunner, placing one foot in front of the other without thinking.

89

Then after an hour or so he started to feel better and just a quickly as it started it was all gone. Obviously it was just some passing malady, typical of the tropics. "Thank God for that"' he thought.

But this was no passing thing it was only the beginning, the calm before the storm. After perhaps half an hour, he noticed that he couldn't look at the sunlight that filtered through the jungle canopy. Each ray of sunlight seemed to burn through his skull like a laser and he would feel dizzy, on the verge of passing out.

Then he noticed that suddenly, he felt very cold, his veins became like rivers of ice with the carotid artery pulsating rapidly, pumping shards of ice directly into his brain. His teeth started to chatter like a pair of castanets, as his mouth became bone dry and his head wanted to burst. His joints were a series of extreme pain between the head and the feet, as he started to shake all over. He heard the distant voice of the medic:

"Shit! He is close to forty one degrees we better get him out ASAP".

"Hey, if my temperature is forty one why am I so cold?".... "I mean this is the hot season, it is stinking hot so why am I so bloody cold?" "Jesus, it is really bloody cold".

After two hours waiting for the "Medivac" helicopter, he was semi conscious, not caring if he lived or died, although by now dying seemed a reasonable way out, no more sensation, no more cold. Finally he felt rather than heard the thumping of the helicopter rotor blades as it hovered above the jungle canopy and lowered the winch with a "Jungle Penetrator" attached to the end. A device, which would allow helicopter evacuation whenever there was no space for it to land.

This device had three metal leaves about a metre in length. Each placed a third of the of the circumference apart which could be folded out and would allow the soldier being evacuated to sit on one and place his legs over the other two as the soldier was being winched up.

90

At the time the Jungle Penetrator was a new device and most soldiers were unfamiliar with the device. Thinking that it would be easier to enter the helicopter by standing on the "Jungle Penetrator", the platoon sergeant told the shivering soldier to hold onto the winch cable and stand on the Penetrator, rather than sit.

Initially everything went well even though the soldier could barely coordinate his movements. It wasn't until he reached the jungle canopy that things became more interesting for everybody. As he ascended through the trees, he felt the branches pulling at him and destabilising his position. By this stage he was about forty feet above the ground and he could see the startled looks of his mates on the ground, with tree canopy playing an active part in preventing his rescue.

In one final attempt a large branch came across both arms as he hung on desperately, which created a pendulum effect and nearly succeeded in tearing him off the "Penetrator", as he cleared the last of the trees and looked up at the helicopter where a rather surprised crewman was waiting to haul him inside.

"What the fuck are you doing?" yelled the crewman, as he hauled him into the helicopter, "You are supposed to sit on it".
"Yeah, well I'm pretty well fucked", replied the barely conscious soldier as he gave the crewman a glazed stare.
"Well you'll know for next time", said the crewman with a smile.

It was short trip of around 20 minutes to the field hospital, where he arrived filthy and covered in sweat, like an unwashed dish cloth, moaning with the pain of being so cold, pleading for a blanket as they take him inside. "I'm fucking freezing", he screamed. His pleas falling on deaf ears, for they well knew that for this infantryman, the torture was just beginning.

By now his temperature was 41 Celsius and the only way to stop his brain from frying and bring his temperature down as quickly as possible, was to place him into a bath of water and ice.

So the unsuspecting soldier who had seen and dealt with eight months of jungle warfare in the tropics with all that came with that, was about to be broken with an Arctic compensation.

Nothing was said as the medical orderlies lowered him gently into the icy water and the only thing the infantry soldier heard is his own scream, "You lousy fucking bastards", as he struggled with the last of his energy while the medics held him down. It would be like this for the next forty-eight hours. He would be subjected to more of the same, as he went through a surreal journey of the past, present and future, each with an ice cold bath and the tremors that followed.

During his last arctic night, he spent another year in Vietnam. The phantoms of the last months came together in a series of disconnected hallucinations. It was a bizarre kaleidoscope of recent experiences. At one point he and a North Vietnamese soldier were taking turns throwing a stick for one of the tracker dogs to chase and bring back. Then, the Vietnamese gave him a blanket to stay warm.

Finally on the morning of the third day he was through on to the other side. His voyage into the freezing, feverish contradiction that is Malaria was over. He had completed one of the coldest voyages one can make, but would remain forever afraid of a recurrence, since the Malarial parasite could remain in the liver for years, waiting for the right conditions to multiply yet again.

Although subsequent bouts of malaria are normally less severe than the previous ones, it is still a reminder of the freezing hell where one would happily be the devil's helper just to avoid those rivers of ice.

12

BRIGHT IDEAS

(That killed the wrong people)

In 1967 the Americans put together a group of top academic scientists known as the Jasons, after Jason and the Argonauts who took a mythological trip into the unknown. However, this new group of Argonauts would develop ideas that seemed not so much unknown but right off the planet.

Their first idea was to build what would be called the McNamara Line, which would be 160 kilometres long and 10 metres wide consisting of stretches of barbed wire studded with mines, chemical weapons and sensor devices. Designed to block the movement of North Vietnamese across the 17th Parallel which divided North and South Vietnam. Along this strip, would be huge areas of free fire-zones that had been denuded of forest cover in yet another bright idea - "Operation Ranch Hand" which used a herbicide known as "Agent Orange", whose notoriety would become public knowledge in years to come.

Eventually the Jasons would settle for a line 60 miles long to be built within a year. It would be protected by small gravel mines that would explode when they were stepped on or run over by a truck. Interspersed between these would be smaller button mines the size of a golf ball, which would blow off a finger or a toe. Any explosion would be picked up by acoustic sensors. These would be monitored by patrol aircraft flying overhead who would in turn drop cluster bombs containing baseball sized bomblets.

The Jasons reckoned that 240 million gravel mines, 300 million button mines and 120,000 cluster bombs a year would do the job at a cost of one billion dollars. Roughly the cost for 3 years of the war.

Unfortunately, the mines could not tell the difference between a human being and a wild animal. As a consequence there were many contact reports, in which air strikes were called down, upon a dog or hapless water buffalo.

The Jasons were not discouraged. They experimented with bed bugs, which were known to be inactive, until a human body came into the vicinity. At which point they would move excitedly at the prospect of a meal. Electrodes that would detect movement were to be glued on the backs of the bed bugs. In fact the bugs were actually spread over the Demilitarised Zone (DMZ). Unfortunately, either the bugs did not take to the jungle or the glue melted but not before more than a million dollars was spent.

Another idea developed by the Jasons was a pigeon borne bomb that would explode when it (the pigeon) landed on a truck. Early in the trial work, it became apparent that this was a no brainer when nobody could train the pigeons to figure out the difference between a Communist and a non-Communist truck.

This obsession with the use of animals reached the height of absurdity, when a General from Central Command, suggested placing Piranha fish from the Amazon River into the rice paddies of Vietnam. This was to be done during the harvest season, with the hope of having the Piranhas attack the hapless rice farmers and thus stopping the rice harvest. This sounded great until someone pointed out that Piranhas needed moving water like a river otherwise they would die.

The final piece of ingenuity was the development of "Turdsid". This was a sensor disguised as a pile of dog excrement. However this was quickly dropped after an Air Cavalry commander pointed out that "While a bear might shit in the woods, there was no evidence of dogs doing so in the jungles of South East Asia".

There were however some ideas that did work. The "Daisy Cutter", a massive bomb that exploded as an air burst causing extensive damage as it cut a swathe of destruction across a wide area.

A useful weapon, if you can ignore the "collateral damage". Some of the acoustic sensors to track enemy movement actually worked. In 1970, a recording from one of the device was played for a committee of the American Congress. The committee heard a conversation in Vietnamese, followed by the sound of axes chopping down the tree on which the device had been snagged. Then there was a crash followed by screams as the tree fell on the men below. Obviously after this type of incident, the NVA were well aware of the sensors and nearly all the information gained was compromised.

The McNamara Line never really worked. It proved impossible to construct properly due to the continual artillery and mortar barrages from the NVA, apart from the fact that the NVA took the obvious and sensible option of going around the line via Laos.

The idea was finally discredited in 1968, when the Marines were besieged at Khe Sanh, just South of the McNamara Line. There the American Marines took casualties reminiscent of World War 1 and despite a courageous effort, were no match for those scrawny little men in black pyjamas. After which the project was scrapped, at a cost of several million dollars and dozens of casualties in the attempted reconstruction.

One of the most ironic bright ideas came from one of Australia's most senior commanders. While every war is unique with its own particular battle problems, the characteristic errors of Vietnam often revolved around the application of conventional tactics to deal with an unconventional war, sometimes leading to situations more suited to Monty Python than guerrilla warfare. In fact some of the greatest problems in Vietnam where caused by the solutions offered.

The worst example of this was an idea dreamt up by one Brigadier Stuart Graham who, like most high ranking officers, tended to fight the war of the day with the tactics of yesterday. That is to say the tactics they used when they last saw action.

With an idea more suited to the Second World War, Brigadier Graham decided to undertake the construction of a minefield, some eleven kilometres in length, from a hill known as "The Horseshoe" down to the coast. The aim of this was to create a barrier denying Mr. Charles access to the villages further south, by laying 23,000 "Jumping Jack" mines.

These mines were the latest in American technology, so called because they came with a primary charge which propelled the mine upwards to a height of about one metre, when the secondary or main charge would detonate the mine. The object of these mines was not so much to kill but rather to wound as many as possible, which require many more resources to extract and care for them. Needless to say, as an added bonus, there was the enormous damage to morale.

Brigadier Graham had seen war service 20 years earlier in World War 2 and prior to his arrival in Vietnam had been the Director of Military Intelligence. The unfolding debacle of the minefield seemed to underline the old joke that military intelligence is an oxymoron, with the Americans referring ironically to Brigadier Graham, as the "Intelligence Brigadier". Against all the advice he received from his predecessor and his battalion commanders, Brigadier Graham pushed ahead with this idea, which became his obsession. The price of which would be paid for by the some 290 Australian casualties, 46 of who were killed or died of wounds.

As the fencing and laying of the minefield commenced, the Army Engineers noticed that children had started flying kites on taller buildings overlooking the minefield, so Charlie was dealing with the threat before it was born. The engineers would lay the mines during the day and the Gooks would dig up what they could at night. As a consequence it was decided to place anti-lift devices underneath the mines, which consisted of a pressure release switch that would set off a hand grenade with an instantaneous fuse placed underneath the mine. Initially, the Charlie took a few casualties when they set off the anti-lift devices. However, once they figured out how to lift both of them together and neutralise the hand grenade, they finished up with a "two for one special" at Brigadier Graham's minefield supermarket.

The Australian Engineers of 1 Field Squadron were placed under enormous pressure to lay an increasing number of mines per day. This was required from mine laying teams who had no experience with this new ordinance. Training in Australia consisted of looking at a schematic diagram of the mine, followed by "on the job" training in Vietnam, which included the highly dangerous task of placing the anti-lift devices. The Australian Engineers managed to increase the number of mines laid from 300 per day to 500 then to 1,000 mines a day, a massive workload under incredibly difficult conditions in a minefield in Vietnam. There is no doubt that this, combined with the terrible heat, wearing flak jackets and steel helmets, led to an increased risk of casualties. Added to this, was the constant threat of enemy action as well as some creative tactics by Charlie, such as the night when buffaloes were pushed into the minefield detonating several mines.

Following one of these "Buffalo Incursions", an officer and sergeant from the engineers undertook the rather hazardous task of going back into the minefield, to replace the mines detonated by the buffaloes. They had just started when another ten mines were set off in rapid succession, as a dog was put in and ran alongside the fence hitting trip wires ahead of the exploding mines. Both of them were peppered with shrapnel but avoided serious injury. This led to the establishment of procedures so that snipers could be posted to deal with the new "enemy", while the engineers continued to lay the minefield.

That was the thing about Vietnam, after a while you began to feel everyone and everything was against you, not only the Viet Cong with their weapons, tunnels and booby traps but their dogs and buffaloes as well. In fact, the land mine could be seen as neutral, it just sat there minding its own business waiting for someone, anyone, to stand on it.

Eventually all the pressure on the Engineers to lay more mines, began to tell and the inevitable happened, when in May of 1967 a series of "Mine Accidents" occurred in which five engineers were killed and six wounded. One of them was sapper Jethro Thompson, a plant operator driving a bull dozer in a land clearing operation, when suddenly, he was sent to the minefield without any familiarisation. Never-the-less he started work until he was badly wounded. As he recounted years later; "Since we had armed our quota of mines, I was surprised to learn that rather than be rotated to another task we were to go back to arming. I was standing there adjusting my flak jacket and looking at my partner Ashley Culkin crouching over a mine in the ground.

I thought, 'Oh shit' he's already into it. And that's the last thing I remember seeing before I was flying through the air. All the dust and crap seemed to float down, covering me in very slow motion. My hands were spewing blood and I could not feel my left leg, actually it felt as if it was hanging over an edge, dangling there, shreds of flesh attached it. My dick was longer than my left leg and I'm not boasting!" "My buttocks and right leg were badly lacerated and left eardrum was perforated. I took a penetrating abdominal wound, which had exposed my intestines. I heard someone yelling out to put the safety pins back in the mines near us. Then one bloke said, 'we can't, Jethro's got them.' Bret Nolen was hovering over me trying to stop the flow of blood. I was hot and looking into the sun".

Miraculously, Jethro lived to tell the tale, while the engineers went back to work the same day. In spite of this disaster the minefield was completed with the 23,000 mines laid in less than a month. From then on for over two years, the Australians provided

Mr. Charles with an excellent ordinance resource, which he used very effectively against them.

In early1969 Australian Command decided to clear and take out all the mines, before Charlie did the job for them. This would take longer and cause even more casualties than it did lay the minefield. By July of 1969 work had commenced to clear the minefield when coincidently, the Trackers were deployed to help secure an FSB into an area known as the "Light Green", notorious for the number of mines which Charlie had replanted from the Australian minefield. One morning in July of 1969 the Trackers were in the FSB, listening to transistor radios as the moon landing was about to be broadcast. Then a sort of instinctive hush came over the FSB. It seemed to start from the radio centre in the middle. Like a stone thrown into a lake, the news rippled outwards, from one section to another, with the news we didn't want to hear. To paraphrase a line from Red Gum's "I Was Only Nineteen", which became the unofficial anthem of the Vietnam War, "Frankie kicked a mine, the day that mankind kicked the moon".

Over the company radio the voice of the 3 platoon operator said, "The boss has walked on a mine".
Lt Peter Hines was killed and 18 other members of the platoon wounded when a jumping jack mine exploded. Only one NCO, Corporal John Needs, was left to take charge. Although seriously wounded, the radio operator continued to transmit details of the incident, while Corporal Needs continued to control the situation.
At the same time, the combat engineer team under the command of Corporal Baxter were also wounded. Regardless of this, Baxter and one of his men started clearing the mines to provide safe access until all the wounded had been treated. Still disregarding his own wounds he continued to clear a landing area for the evacuation helicopters. For his extraordinary effort he was awarded the Military Medal.

The battalion mounted a relief operation, with the Commanding Officer David Butler and the Regimental Medical Officer Trevor Anderson at hand during this relief effort. Once the task had been completed and all the casualties evacuated, the CO and the RMO were returning along a path, taped and cleared of mines when someone in the group, stepped on a mine right on the edge of the tape and another mine was triggered.

The doctor was permanently blinded with another six wounded including the CO. Standing some distance away was "Needsie", 3 platoon's only surviving NCO after the first mine explosion. When the second mine exploded "Needsie" dropped like a stone, not moving. The first one to reach him was Warrant Officer "Smiler" Myles, who was about to take over the remnants of 3 Platoon after the first explosion. Warrant Officer "Smiler" Myles described the situation years later.

"Needsie" was lying on the ground with not a mark on him, although it was obvious he had been hit. We tried to find where it had got him so we could patch him up and the only wound we could find was a small hole, straight through his heart". The last of the command structure for 3 platoon was wiped out.

In spite of his wounds and in great pain, Lt Col Butler calmly directed the evacuation of the wounded before accepting any attention for himself. Some weeks later, in a fine example of good leadership, he returned to command the Battalion until the tour of duty was finished nine months later.

The remaining soldiers of 3 platoon were airlifted to company headquarters and that afternoon, a new platoon commander, Lt Peter Marks-Chapman flew in, accompanied by reinforcements. A few hours later, the survivors and the new arrivals checked their equipment, loaded their weapons and as the sun was going down, moved out for an all night ambush patrol. To an outsider, it could seem like handing out a completed death certificate to all participants, for the Australians it was, as one remarked, "Just another day at the office".

This would be the first of a series of mine incidents that occurred over a period of 48 hours, killing 7 and wounding 32 without a shot being fired. After that there was always an added sense of fear whenever they were sent into the "Light Green".

In the Light Green, the sense of fear was deep enough for them to be placing their feet instinctively in the footsteps of others in front. While the forward scouts leading the patrol were often well in front of the section. Obviously this was with the unsaid hope, that if they triggered a mine, there would be fewer casualties. Inevitably they developed a bit of mine neuroses whenever they patrolled "The Light Green".

When they returned to their base at Nui Dat after an operation, with a reasonably large amount of alcohol consumed, occasionally they would play a game stepping from one chair or table to another each with a footprint outlined in chalk. Anyone stepping outside the footprint would be required to drink a can of beer without stopping and buy the next round.

Those "jumping jacks" were always very destructive and very expensive if anyone missed the footprint.

13

THE ESSENCE OF COURAGE

The Trackers, along with the rest of the battalion had just started preparing for a second tour of duty in Vietnam, when Ken and a few other new soldiers arrived to join the platoon. Over the next months they completed their advanced training which included courses in visual tracking, long range patrolling and reconnaissance.

It soon became obvious that Ken had the potential to be more than just a private soldier and in a short space of time Ken was given the job of section 2IC or Lance Corporal. He was more than proficient in his new position and did well with the additional responsibility. A few months later, not long before the battalion's departure for Vietnam, Ken became a section commander. He would be the only section commander in the platoon who had no previous combat experience but this was not unusual and certainly no bar to promotion.

As the Trackers went through the final stages of training, Ken adapted to his new role easily enough and after the novelty wore off, he was accepted by everyone without reservation. In what seemed like the shortest space of time the Trackers were disembarking from the aircraft carrier HMAS Sydney onto the shores of Vietnam.

The atmosphere had changed and like everyone else, Ken could feel the drumbeat of a country at war. Ken found his first patrol was easy enough, patrolling through the relatively quiet area close to Nui Dat. At times he could see the hill which marked the centre of the base and occasionally the sounds of trucks, made that first patrol seem like a walk in the park. If the tour of duty would be like this there wasn't much to fear.

During their second week the Trackers were deployed with one of the rifle companies for a short five day operation. It was during this operation that Ken experienced the absolute exhaustion that comes with jungle warfare in the tropics. This feeling of total exhaustion normally overtakes everyone from about three o'clock in the afternoon onwards. For the ordinary soldier it was a bit easier to deal with, he just had to do as he was told without much thought involved but as a section commander, Ken had to navigate, using map and compass and control the section.

The other factor which played on everyone's mind was that this was no longer a military exercise back in Australia, where everyone was pretending and all the casualties came back to life. This was the real thing, with real bullets and real rockets. Above all else, as a section commander Ken had to set the example, no matter how tired or frightened he may have felt. Aside from the platoon commander or platoon sergeant, probably the most difficult job, is that of an infantry section commander.

If Ken, like everyone else, was beginning to understand this after a short five day warm up operation the obvious question was, "How do we handle one month of this?" This was the time frame for the first major operation. There was some breathing space of about a week before the first operation which allowed everyone to prepare for the first of several exhausting operations, each one lasting about a month.

The Trackers left Nui Dat they feeling confident and rested the exhaustion of the five days in the jungle forgotten, as they raced through the countryside on the armoured personnel carriers, to establish their first fire support base. After securing and establishing the aptly named Fire Support Base "Virginia" (this was after all their first operation) the Trackers started with a series of daily reconnaissance and ambush patrols. After a couple of weeks, everyone was left with accumulated exhaustion, trying to be effective with only five or at the most six hours sleep a night.

By this stage all of the section commanders were finding it difficult to maintain morale and enthusiasm. For Ken it was even more difficult as this was his first experience of war and it was in the second week of the operation that he handled his first dead

Viet Cong who had been shot by one of his section. The reality of war was always magnified by the continuing exhaustion.

The image of the dead VC played on Ken's mind. The last thing he wanted was to finish up like that. The thought and feeling was a continual distraction every time that Ken was on patrol and like everyone else he was counting the days to a good sleep, a shower and clean clothes.

There were about ten days left to complete the operation when, what would be a personal disaster for Ken, occurred late in the afternoon. Ken was looking at his map and wishing that the operation was well and truly over when there was an exchange of fire between Ken's forward scout and a couple of Viet Cong. Ken dropped to the ground behind a log as the VC continued to fire back.

Ken could hear the crack of the incoming rounds above him and placed his rifle on top of the log and started firing blind as he hid behind the log. By firing his rifle in this way the forward scout who was in front of him was obviously in danger of being shot, never mind the rule of war, "You only fire when you can see the enemy". This continued for about fifteen or twenty seconds until the VC broke off contact, but those few seconds would lead to several months of guilt and anguish for Ken and the loss of respect by some of those who knew him.

What Ken didn't know, was that his actions were seen by two others in the section and within hours, the rest of the section had heard about the incident. The story was no doubt exaggerated, not from any malicious intent but because the intensity of combat can never allow war stories to be told without some emotion. It was not that Ken was a coward; rather that he reacted instinctively as everyone does when they are exhausted, particularly when they face the first experience of war.

In his mind Ken felt that he had been tested and failed and from that moment on it was difficult for him not feel that his section had little respect for him, manifested by a sense of quiet discontent. Of course Ken could never raise the subject himself.

105

Just how does a leader bring the ultimate issue of courage or perceived lack of it, into an open discussion, without risking further degradation of his position?

Over the next few weeks, "The Incident" was pretty much forgotten in the fast and furious rhythm of war, although in Ken's mind it was always in the background and every now and then in the quiet moments back in Nui Dat, there would be the odd remark about "looking for logs two metres thick, whenever a contact was imminent".

Of course, eventually matters came to a head just before the third operation, when Ken heard the story about "The Incident" repeated by someone in another unit. The combined feelings of failure, shame and embarrassment, drove him into an absolute black rage.

Ken returned to the Tracker's base determined to find out who was responsible for spreading the story and commenced by questioning anyone who might have seen the "The Incident". Unfortunately one of the lance corporals, Nick, was not in a particularly good mood and very drunk when he was questioned. He responded as he laughed with, "Well, so what if I did say something, everyone knows you like a big tree to hide behind!"

That was the final straw for Ken. He was confronted with the uncomfortable truth of a momentary physical weakness and the only way for him to respond was to fight. Many blows were exchanged, until Ken managed to knock his opponent to the ground, where in his state of madness he started kicking Nick continuously. The head, the stomach, the back, wherever his feet could strike and finally, when Nick could hardly move, Ken walked away, honour satisfied, as far as Ken was concerned.

Eventually Nick stood up unsteadily; bruised and bleeding he staggered into the tent where the other lance corporals were billeted and commenced to load the magazine for his rifle.
"That bastard is going to pay, you know he put the slipper in, he kicked the shit out of me".

The others in the tent weren't too concerned, one of them commenting in a light hearted way, "Look you don't need to load the whole magazine just a couple of rounds is more than enough to kill him".

"Tell ya what pal, I'm going to put the whole magazine into that bastard", replied Nick.

By this point most of the Trackers knew what had happened and they along with Ken were well aware that Nick was looking for him with a loaded rifle. While the rest of the night and the following days passed without incident, it was only because Ken spent that night and the rest of the time away from the Trackers area, to avoid any contact with Nick. His fears were well founded, after all a drunken soldier in a theatre of war with a loaded weapon, who had just been given a savage beating, provides the most likely scenario for a shooting.

With this background even more fear, anger and frustration was created for Ken, as he waited impatiently for the start of the next operation. At least the demands of patrolling would drown the atmosphere of sullen discontent, which was now the predominant mood in his section. Of course for Ken there was the underlying dread that if there was a contact, Charlie could have him ducking for cover and once again Ken would be hiding behind a log face down, firing his rifle over the top, overcome by fear.

Before the next operation there were two days taken up with the usual frenetic activity of preparing equipment and test firing weapons, while Ken maintained a low profile, leaving most of the work to the section 2IC. Every now and then Ken would meet Nick face to face and Nick would give him a smouldering stare full of hate saying, "You're gone pal, you are fucking dead."

Now Ken had two enemies who wanted to kill him, Charlie and Nick; one in front and one behind.

The insertion phase of the next operation was by helicopter, giving a picturesque overview of where they would be hunting Charlie for the next four weeks.

As it turned out the operation was quiet with very few contacts, none of which involved Ken or his section, much to his relief. Although at the start of everyday there was always that feeling of apprehension in the back of Ken's mind, "How will I deal with the next contact?" This personal fear, which every soldier has, was in Ken's mind magnified by his own perceived failure. This was further exacerbated with the obvious change in attitude by his own section towards him in an atmosphere of sullen compliance to his orders. It was with a sense of boredom and exhaustion that the operation was completed.

By this time "The Incident" and subsequent beating of Nick by Ken was a dim memory although, never really forgotten, amongst dozens of other memories that occur in the heightened atmosphere of war. While the animosity between Nick and Ken was always there, after a few weeks it became more of a dull dislike between two people.

Following their return to Nui Dat, the Trackers had a week to rest before starting the next operation. This cycle of a month on operation followed by a week break preparing for the next operation had by now, become the rhythm of life for everybody. Although for Ken there was a something missing, a degree of diffidence from his section and others in the platoon, or was that just his imagination?

Maybe he should apologise to Nick? Maybe Nick was still spreading the story? Or maybe he was just being paranoid. Whatever the case Ken was finding it increasingly difficult to deal with the everyday issues, which come with being a section commander.

The nights were the hardest of all, wether out on patrol or back in Nui Dat, the darkness of the tropical jungle always amplified the fears, real or imagined, lingering, distorting matter-of-fact objects, making them bigger or smaller and sometimes making them move. However the night time distortion of his thoughts was even worse, exacerbating the dark depression, which resulted in an even greater fear of what would happen the next time Ken would have to deal with Charlie.

Of course Charlie was always on everyone's mind but not in the same fearful way that rested in Ken's mind, after all in his mind he had three enemies, those who witnessed "The Incident", his deep fear of repeated failure and Charlie. What Ken couldn't understand was that while his section was well aware of "The Incident" and there may have been some lack of respect, they each had their own problems and fears.

In this frame of mind he concentrated on preparing his equipment for the next operation and last of all, briefing his section. This was done in a mechanical and wooden way, that always seems to exist when there is an elephant in the room that everyone has to ignore.

Two days into the operation the Trackers had their first contact with no result. The Trackers started to follow the sign left behind, with Ken's section in the rear as Charlie moved deeper into the jungle. As they moved further into the jungle there were obvious signs of a bunker system and the platoon stopped while the platoon commander carried out a reconnaissance of the area. He then gave his orders and finished saying, "It looks like we have a few Nogs up ahead so we have to be really careful and Ken, you will be the lead section".

Ken's face showed no emotion, he just turned a whiter shade of pale and said, "Ok boss," as he turned and walked back to his section. This was the moment he had been dreading, Ken felt nauseated with the sinking feeling one has when bad news has been delivered.
He briefed his section and found himself drinking large amounts of water as he spoke, his mouth dry and his heart pounding as he tried to sound in command.

"If you don't have any questions we'll move on to the front of the platoon", he said as he finished his briefing.

After a couple of minutes the section was moving through the rest of the platoon making their way to the front with the scout in the lead followed by Ken and the other eight in the section. For Ken this was no Greek like battle in which he would return, "With his shield or on it". This was sheer terror and there was nothing romantic or adventurous in any of this.

As they followed the track through the thick jungle, Ken could see the unmistakable fresh imprints of Ho Chi Minh sandals, Charlie's favourite footwear, which just added to the sense of danger and in that moment Ken knew that a contact was a few seconds away. It was then that he became enraged.

"You fucking bastards are not going give me any more misery!"

The last two months of sleepless nights, the bashing he gave Nick along with the unnecessarily brutal kicking, all came into his mind along with the absolute fear that existed within. As his anger reached an internal crescendo, two shots were fired by his scout, followed by a burst of machine gun fire.

"Contact Front!" he yelled, as he dropped to the ground.

Then immediately, he started to direct his section to lay down covering fire so that the rest of the platoon could carry out a platoon attack. As the contact started to take some shape, Ken understood that Charlie had to be within a few metres of his scout who couldn't move without being exposed to the machine gun. By now there was no fear in Ken, but a wild enthusiasm fuelled by his anger, through which he found himself raised on one knee from where he could see Charlie behind a mound of dirt and just as he had been trained to do, fired two shots which flung the VC backwards.

By now, the rest of the platoon had started their sweep across the front of Ken's section, looking for any more of Charlie's friends and when the area was cleared, Ken and his scout moved forward to search the body of the dead VC.

As the scout rolled the dead VC over, he saw the two small holes of the entry wound. "Not a bad shot, straight through the chest; thanks, I owe you for that", he said to Ken.

110

"Let's just say that we're even", replied Ken with a wry smile as he as he signalled the rest of his section to move up.

That night, after they had settled into a night time defensive position, in spite of the contact hours before, Ken was the most relaxed he had been since arriving in Vietnam.

Years later, to those who knew about it, "The Incident" became irrelevant and with the wisdom of years they all understood, that overcoming failure is not as spectacular as physical courage.

It is in fact, the essence of courage.

14

GOING TROPPO

"The worst way to be in this place, is sane"
Advice to a new arrival in Vietnam

Operations would normally last about a month, so that by the time they came back to Nui Dat, the six-man tents would be taken over by insects of every possible type. From the fiery red ants, to the less vicious but larger black ants which all moved in battalions and mosquitoes that always seemed to fly in squadrons.

Sometimes as an added bonus, there were nests of wasps to complement the centipedes, spiders and beetles. Some of these would feed on each other depending on how high up the food chain they were, others seemed to survive on nothing but dust.

The first night back in base after nearly a month away was always a challenge. The soldiers had to fight and retake their territory from the insects. The chorus of insect noises being broken up with the sounds of scratching, swearing and, of course, the continual pfsssst, pfsssst, pfsssst of fly spray, a fly spray which these days is banned, due to its carcinogenic properties.

There was always the battle against one of their really dangerous enemies the mosquito which carried the malarial parasite. The mosquito net would be well placed and secured until a high-pitched buzzing would announce that the net had been breached. This would be followed by a predictable series of events swearing, a long pfsssst as the spray was used and torchlight to locate and close the breach. During the wet season a mattress would become a source of large black ants, very friendly lice and a pungent odour, which emanated from the thick patches of green mould.

Normally two or three days were needed to re-establish supremacy over the insects. This meant that there would be at least two nights with very little sleep. This was the most sought after commodity, especially after weeks of patrolling for ten hours a day, carrying those bloody heavy packs, looking for Charlie.

The exhaustion enveloped everyone, with the tropical humidity acting like a hot wet blanket, forcing everyone to move in slow motion. At least back at the base they were safe, or as safe as anyone could be in Vietnam. Surrounded with barbed wire, machine guns, mortars and artillery, they could relax, except of course for the fresh memories of the operation just completed. For a few, there was the searing memory of killing another human being, with the instinctive knowledge that something was broken forever. After killing someone, an intrinsic part of humanity was lost. From that day on they could justify anything done to anybody, short of killing, by the fact that they were allowed to live.

For others it was the memory of a near miss, or rather a near hit would be a better description, which was occasionally associated with the ultimate oxymoron, of "Friendly Fire". And anyone who has been on the receiving end of this will know that it is anything but friendly. Sometimes there was that stroke of luck that made them late thereby missing the helicopter that went down. With all of these memories to choose from, combined with the odd angry shot, the heat, humidity and lack of sleep, little wonder that the brain could become unhinged and on occasions one went "Troppo".

After all, every time one sees death, there is the penalty, which is called memory and under these conditions, alcohol was not an option but rather a necessity. Never mind that alcohol exacerbates the negativity, for a short while, it helps to forget the memories and dulls the pain, a cheap and cheerful route to oblivion. There were three key rules to survival in Vietnam, the first was never run out of alcohol, and the other two rules were the same as the first.

Many of the soldiers living in this small piece of Australia located in South Vietnam were idealists, true believers who thought it was right to be in this war. There were even "Nashos" who had volunteered for the draft. By definition they had to be idealists of a certain type, to volunteer to live in this fine line between lunacy and insanity. Yes, it was possible to live between these two forms of "Normal" behaviour that existed in Nui Dat. Perhaps they could have been considered, in a positive sense, misfits young people who never really fitted in back home and this was their way of escaping reality, although no one spoke that truth.

However, by the time they had completed 4 months of operations, they would have found Joseph Hellers "Catch 22" more than appropriate and quite rational if one had a concern for objective and immediate danger. The rationale was quite simple. One could refuse to go out on a patrol if he was crazy and if one claimed that the mission was crazy, or too dangerous, then that was obviously sane and rational thinking. In which case he wasn't crazy and therefore was capable of going out on patrol. Basically if one refused to go out on patrol, then he was obviously sane and had to go. In fact the crazies had no problems they were just fine. It was the sane who had the problems. They to deal with the fact that they were being driven insane and they did it by deciding that until they died, they were invincible and would live forever and so far they were doing just fine.

Going out on patrol was made worse when they came to realise that the problem was not so much the VC or the NVA, rather it was the villager who waved at them as they passed by and then shot at them the next day. That was the reality of Vietnam.

Eventually in this mix of humanity they created their own social rules in the micro society of Nui Dat, a place that few in the world knew existed, unless they were connected to someone there. It was a place of contradictions on a daily basis. Social drinking and the quantity consumed depend on the type of society in which this is done. In Nui Dat it was generally accepted that once everyone was lolling around in their chairs like elderly pensioners at an Alzheimer's convention, they had consumed enough. All of this taking place, while the army chaplains were extolling the dangers of alcohol. Never mind that one of the chaplains was a functioning alcoholic.

Then there was gambling in the company mess hall, until ten in the evening as if they were back home, followed around midnight, by the occasional rocket or mortar from Mr. Charles, just to remind them that their ideals would always be tested. At that point, often the "safe place" they thought they were in, would seem like a prison.

By the last two months of the tour, they learned to dread one day at a time, just to make it back home was all they wanted. Some of this was reflected in a song by "The Animals" that by the end had became their anthem, "We gotta get outta this place" (if it's the last thing we ever do), that was played repeatedly, as they crossed off the numbered days on a computer generated outline of a naked woman, with the number 365 on the vital Going Home spot or G spot.

With this insane mix in the background, the first night back in base always involved some serious drinking which for some like Crazy Kev meant at least a dozen cans of beer and a few whisky chasers. The result was that next morning he was standing in line at the mess hall nursing a huge hangover, very, very tired and extremely irritable. Army food has never been known for its high standard a la the "Michelin Guide" and the army never really understood that soldiers needed a balanced diet. It seemed happy just to deliver calories for energy regardless of presentation or taste and that's how the day started off badly for "Crazy Kev".

To top off a night of no sleep with a huge hangover and a severe ear infection, there was the sloppy porridge, followed by greasy eggs and "Spam" sliding around in oil. For the uninitiated, in the army, "Spam" is an acronym for "Shit Posing as Meat" and true to form, the Army Catering Corps developed an exceptionally creative cuisine for the masses. The Spam would be thickly sliced then deep-fried until there was a crisp dark brown outer layer. This required a sawing motion to bite through a piece at which point two or three large globules of fat would burst into the mouth, leaving a layer of grease over the tongue, which could be washed down with dark sickly sweet stewed tea. Knowing from past experience what was before him Crazy Kev was not at all happy. "What is this crap?" said to nobody in particular.

Now, over the centuries, soldiers have always complained about the food they were given, in most cases justifiably so and "Crazy Kev" or CK as he was known, had good reason for his complaint. What made CK different was his capacity to give real meaning to his complaint and while some of the others came close to knowing him, they never crossed that border. This was probably a good thing since it might have made CK an enemy for everyone and that was the last thing they needed. The thing was that CK had the disconcerting habit of always having a machete handy twenty-four hours a day and slept with it drawn at night. There were several stories (no doubt exaggerated) from others in the platoon, who had woken CK in the middle of the night for sentry duty. Only to be confronted by a blood curdling yell and a maniacal CK waking up, machete in hand, ready to take on all comers in whatever threat was there, imagined or real. With phrases like: "Ya faarking baastards! C'mon, I'll faarkin ave ya!"

Needless to say, if the rest of the platoon was having a mildly nervous night, in the jungles of wartime Vietnam, CK was able to single handedly transform that nervousness, into a night of sheer terror for the whole platoon. In the process ruining any chance of sleep.

Of course nobody said anything to him, particularly after his dissertation on how useful the machete was.

"You blokes don't know just how good it is, you can use it for clearing the way, opening beer bottles, digging shallow holes with the back of it and if the fire support base was overrun you could use it as the "Final Fucking Solution", I'm telling you, I don't go to sleep without it".

After a couple of months, if anyone had to wake up CK, they did so with the utmost caution, from at least two or three metres away, normally by throwing small stones at him. In spite of all this, he was probably one of the best machine gunners in the company and completely fearless, always there when he was needed.

With this background, after months of very ordinary food, Crazy Kev decided to pass on his unsolicited but expert opinion, of "Haute Cuisine a la Militaire" to the cook, with a sophisticated opening.

"Are you the pogo fuckhead who cooked this crap?" he asked the newly arrived cook.

"Well who the fuck are you?" replied the cook.

"I'm one of the blokes who has to eat this shit", said Crazy Kev.

"Yeah, well if you reckon you can do a better job why don't you give it a go?" said the unsuspecting cook.

"Right ya faarking bastard!" yelled Crazy Kev as he leapt over the food counter, picking up a heavy metal soup ladle as he landed on the other side. The hapless cook started to turn and run when CK whacked him on the head, leaving him stunned on the floor. After months of continuous violence in Vietnam, a half-stunned cook was no big deal, it wasn't as though CK had killed him and everyone knew better than to intervene on the cook's behalf.

So there was Crazy Kev, astride the stunned cook metal soup ladle in hand, shaking all over with a combination of rage, born in a large part from the fears and frustrations of weeks in the jungle and the remnants of the previous nights alcohol coursing through his veins. At this point there was the distinct possibility of a riot between the Grunts on one side, and the Tucker Fuckers, as the cooks were known, on the other side.

While Crazy Kev's assessment of the food may have been correct, to prevent the situation from getting out of hand, the most senior NCO's became involved and after a couple of hours a truce was arranged, whereby Crazy Kev agreed to apologise, provided the mess could be named by the Grunts. A seemingly irrelevant concession, however these small things become very important when someone "Goes Troppo"

So it was that the mess was named, not inappropriately given the quality of food served, "Chew it and Spew it", and Crazy Kev would smile, every time he walked in for a meal.

Photographs

The following photographs were taken by these 6RAR Trackers

6RAR Trackers (painted by T Woodward)	John Neervoort
Tracker group	John Neervoort
Chew It & Spew It	Bill Kromwyk
Skull Cave	Rick Robinson
Skull & dog handlers	Bruce Williams
69 Bar Vung Tau	Don 'Jock' Bain
Crashed Chinook	Bruce Williams
Forward Scout	'Mooka' McDonald
Bushranger gunship	Bruce Williams
Three stooges	Bruce Williams
Piper	Bill Kromwyk
Flag on Nui May Tao	Tony Hersey
Bushman Scout	Dick Barry
Milo with beer	John Neervoort
Anti-Tank Tracker sign (painted T Woodward)	John Neervoort

Home beneath the rubber trees at Nui Dat

The Trackers preparing for a patrol

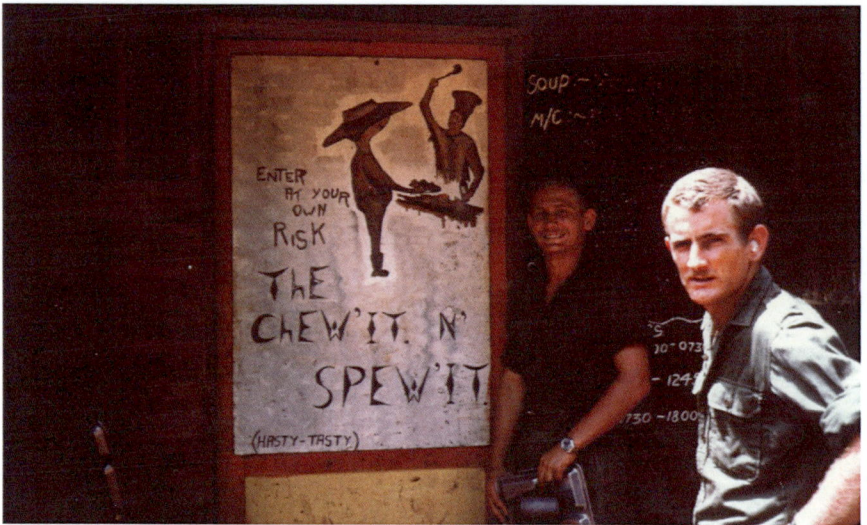

The name says it all - Chew It and Spew It

The Skull Cave

Charlie and his friends

Fiery red tree ants

The burnt remains of the crashed Chinook helicopter

The forward scout on the edge of a clearing

An Australian Huey helicopter gunship

Never take life very seriously

The pipe major playing the bagpipes

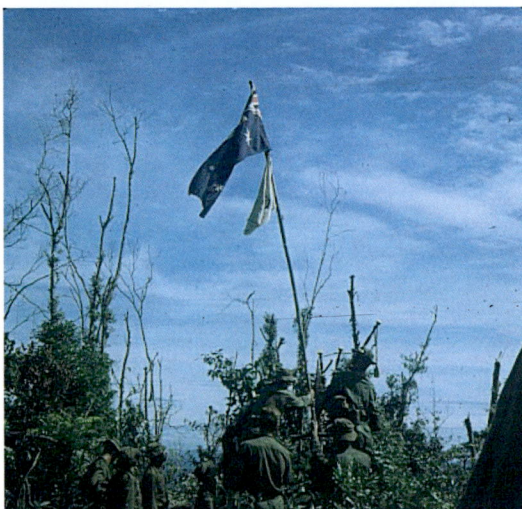

as the flag is raised on Nui May Tao

Nguyen Xuan Tinh, Bushman Scout

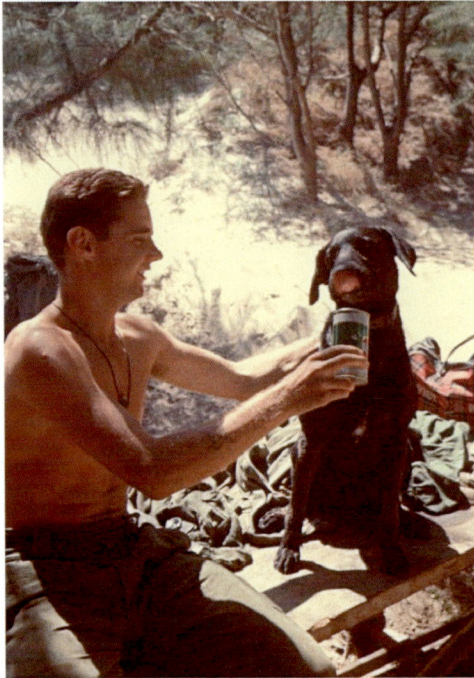

Willy giving Milo a birthday beer

ANTI-TANK VI TRACKER PL.

YOU LOSE EM', WELL FIND EM'

15

NEVER TAKE LIFE VERY SERIOUSLY

"Life is too important to be taken very seriously"
Oscar Wilde

It was a hot and sticky February afternoon, when the replacement section commander arrived. The previous one had been killed two days earlier, when someone stood on a deadly "Jumping Jack" mine, which resulted in another eight casualties.

These mines had a primary charge which would send the mine up to waist height, followed by the deadly secondary charge which sprayed shrapnel in all directions, designed to kill and maim as many as possible. Ironically, the mines had originally been laid by the Australians to try and restrict the movement of Mr. Charles. As usual he adapted very quickly to this potential threat, by digging up the mines and placing them elsewhere, thereby creating an endless supply for his own use. A very Buddhist take on, "What goes around comes around".

Two soldiers were packing the dead Corporal's personal gear into a Land Rover, as the new section commander placed his pack at the entrance of the tent.

"G'Day, you blokes with 3 platoon?" he asked, lighting a cigarette.

"Yup", said the shorter of the two. "And you'd be the new section commander, right?"

"Yeah, I've got 3 Section," he said, trying not to show the newness of his appointment.

"Well, I'm your 2IC", said the tall thin lance corporal with mousy coloured hair, "The name's David but they call me Fang", he paused, "Like, I don't eat much and this is Shorty, he's our machine gunner".

"Right", he said, as he shook hands with both of them, "So where are the rest of the blokes?"

"Well, they're down at the canteen having a few drinks; most of them are new in country, so they're pretty fucked up after the mine incident". Fang paused, looking at the dead corporal's gear.

"Fact is we only have two originals left out of a platoon of thirty two, we've had a total of thirty eight casualties in the last nine months".

At this point Shorty interjected with a shake of the head, "Yeah, and the bloke you're replacing lasted ten weeks", he said, as if to underline the reputation of 3 Platoon as the battalion's bad luck mascot. The fact that their radio call sign one-three, was the same as thirteen just added to the bleak ambience, of low morale that came with the extraordinarily high casualties suffered by 3 Platoon.

"How about you blokes, how long you been here?" asked the section commander.

"We both arrived five months ago", replied Shorty. "Which makes us pretty senior", he said with a wry smile.

"And lucky", replied the section commander ironically. Not wanting to underscore the negative issue of casualties, he continued, "OK, Fang, once you've finished cleaning up, tell the rest of the section to be here at 1500hrs for a briefing. I've got an orders group with the platoon commander in a couple of hours, for our next operation".

"Right, I'll let them know and umm, aahh well," he said hesitating, looking at the dead corporal's photos and letters on the bed, then continued "Are you ok to use this bed or ummm?"

"Yeah, better than the floor isn't it?" replied the section commander, trying to lighten the atmosphere created by the awkward choice of a dead man's bed or the floor.

Later that afternoon in February of 1970, orders were given for a search and destroy operation along the Sui Giao River. Where Military Intelligence suggested there may be more than one hundred enemy, with heavy weapons in a bunker system. Although a review of the American and Australian experience in Vietnam to date, would render the concept of Military Intelligence oxymoronic. Since often many of the assessments were a calculated guess, the usual definite maybe, containing neither rhyme nor reason.

There was anything but logic, with the idea of sending an under strength platoon, to verify the existence of over one hundred enemy in a bunker system. If anything this tended to underline the probability as very remote. It was with this atmosphere of doubtful and underestimated intelligence that the operation started in February 1970. The majority of soldiers in the platoon were reinforcements, with no experience in combat operations and a new platoon commander, the previous two having been killed in action. By the afternoon of the third day, everyone was exhausted, thirsty and fed up, with chasing after yet another phantom in black pyjamas, which was Charlie.

The section commander moved his section in front of the platoon, in single file along a ridgeline. They started to move across a small clearing, when there was a burst of automatic fire from a Kalashnikov. Now they had certainty.

The adrenalin was pumping as everyone moved into the contact drill. Was it a just a sniper or was it a sentry for an enemy bunker system? Everyone had their senses stretched to the limit as they searched for Charlie.

"Where is he? Can you see him?" yelled the section commander.

There was no reply from his forward scout, Dave Wilson. After a few seconds, he saw that twenty metres in front, his forward scout was lying on the ground, not moving.

"Oh shit no!"

"C'mon move! Get up here!" He needed an extended line, to put in as much fire as possible towards the enemy and he needed it quickly. Dave still hadn't moved.

"Oh bloody hell, hurry up!"

Then, on his right, he saw Shorty Jeffries and two others with the machine gun, then the rest of the section on his left.

"Jesus Christ" he thought, "Now it's the moment of truth and I'm scared". This drill entailed the section laying down covering fire, while he moved forward to bring the scout back.

"Are you going or not?" yelled Jeffries.

He was truly scared and his hands were shaking, he really did not want to do this.

"Ok, ok I'm going in", he replied. "Start covering fire on the count of three".

Now everything was in narrow focus. It's a simple task he thought, just run forward twenty metres, pick up Dave and run back and hope that there would be enough covering fire to stop any Nogs from having a go.

He yelled out the numbers, just as they were taught in training, "One, two, threeee!"

Twenty metres never seemed so long. The covering fire reached a crescendo when he picked up Dave, who started screaming as they staggered back to some low ground behind the line of fire. As they hit the ground, the reason for Dave's screams became obvious. He had at least two rounds in the upper left thigh and a large gaping wound which exposed part of his femur as if someone had excised his thigh with a chain saw.

"Don't worry, the dust-off chopper is on the way, you're going to make it", said the section commander, trying to reassure him, although the look on his face would have shown the lie. The medic took over, while the others covered the platoon sweep across the front. As usual, Mr. Charles had vanished.

They had a few minutes rest before moving forward. Nearly everyone was smoking nervously, guzzling water between puffs, Christ! They were always so thirsty after a contact. The section commander could hear Dave moaning in the background and felt the build up of anger and fear. The sun was low in the sky as the section moved forward to meet the platoon commander and the radio operator while the platoon sergeant and the medic waited with Dave Wilson for the dust-off helicopter.

The section commander was ordered to move his section forward when he noticed two large banana leaves on the ground, about eight metres in front of them.

There were no banana trees nearby.

The implication dawned on him, just as one of the leaves was raised as if by an invisible cord and underneath he saw a pair of eyes looking at him. He froze in surprise, too stunned for any reaction as the leaf descended. Then, with a combination of rage and fear for the VC who had shot his scout, bought his rifle to the shoulder and fired four deliberately aimed shots. The rounds punched the Viet Cong backwards, as he fired back with his Kalashnikov, narrowly missing the platoon commander.

This was followed by deafening silence, with all of them lying on the ground looking at each other. With the unsaid question, "was he dead"? The usual answer, maybe. One of the riflemen yelled out, "I've got a grenade". Seconds later, the force of the explosion shuddered through the ground, as the grenade put a definitive end to the life of a brave enemy sentry.

They moved down and joined the rest of the platoon as the tail-end section and started moving forward with another section taking the lead. After moving less than two hundred metres there was an eruption of machine-gun fire and rocket propelled grenades. Almost immediately, forward movement became impossible.

"Looks like we've found the bunker system," said Fang, as if he were discussing the weather.

Suddenly Charlie was firing from both sides, indicating that all three sections had unknowingly penetrated the bunker system and were now caught in a crossfire. The platoon commander came stumbling back with blood streaming from a head wound. "We've lost the radio operator", he said, "And the lead section is stuck".

Misunderstanding him, the section commander said, "What do you mean fucked?"

"Stuck, I said stuck", replied the platoon commander, like piece of black comedy.

"What's the difference", he thought, they were still in deep trouble.

At that point the platoon commander ordered the section commander forward, to deal with the rocket fire. As the section moved forward, one of the riflemen from the lead section came crawling back, his legs covered in blood.

"What's happening up front?" asked the section commander.

"I don't know, I don't know," he replied, "There are a lot of wounded". The look in his eyes was a combination of fear and pain. He was a replacement who had left Australia three weeks before, to replace another casualty. This would be his first and last contact; he would be going home.

A few metres further on they found the radio operator unconscious with shrapnel wounds to his head and right shoulder. There was no reaction as the section commander took the radio off his back and started speaking with the company commander, while one of the riflemen gave first aid to the radio operator.

"We have about nine down", said the section commander, trying to sound in control. (The figure was a guess. In the end the total would be fourteen)

"Where is Sunray?" asked the company commander, using the radio designation for a commander.

"Sunray is down and we are requesting Dustoff", he replied.

"Your Dustoff is on the way, pass me Sunray"

"Passing now, wait out" he said running back to the platoon commander. As he gave him the radio, once again his section was ordered forward, this time to help withdraw the forward elements of the platoon.

As they made their way up to the forward section, he looked back and saw one of his riflemen, who was sitting against a tree moaning, with the centre section of his nose and part of his eye socket shot away, he was unable to see anything. In an act of "mateship", one of the other wounded saw his predicament and returned to take his hand and guide him back.

At the forward edge of the contact they accounted for everybody except the machine gunner from the lead section, who was pinned down by two VC firing rockets at him.

"I think I can see them", said Fang.

Just then there was a huge explosion as a rocket hit the tree above Fang, who took most of the blast and some shrapnel. Surprisingly, he was still quite lucid and able to function.

A few seconds later the machine gunner called out "They're moving on you're left"

"Where are they?" yelled the section commander.

"I don't know, but if you stand up you can probably see them".

So in an act of blind rage for his destroyed section, he got up on one knee and saw two VC about thirty metres away ready to fire another rocket. He fired a long burst which sorted out the Nog with the rocket launcher.

Then, all of a sudden, he glimpsed the tell tale sign of dust being kicked up by a light machine gun on his left and felt a massive thud in the hip which spun him around, with his rifle falling from his hands. Dazed and on the ground for some seconds, he was unable to comprehend what had happened. Until he saw the blood pouring down his thigh. He had been shot.

127

"Oh fuck no! They've got me", he thought as he tried frantically to move his leg and look for his rifle at the same time, feeling naked without it. Finally he saw it a couple of metres away and crawled across to pick it up. As he picked it up, the machine gunner from the lead section came crashing through the bushes.

"Thanks, I thought I was done", gasped the machine gunner.

Amazingly, after at least four rockets fired at the machine gunner, he had emerged without a scratch. The others however, were not in good shape. Strangely enough, nobody complained of any pain, perhaps they were overwhelmed by the knowledge that they still had to get out of the bunker system in the growing darkness, with Charlie all over the place.

Using fire and movement, covering each other, it took them more than an hour to fight their way back 300 metres, to the relative safety of the dust-off area. Towards the end of the withdrawal from the bunker system, the situation had become rather desperate as they were running out of ammunition. By the time they reached the dust-off area, some had less than 20 rounds of ammunition left. Each of them had fired more than 150 rounds each in the last two hours

The scene at the dust-off area could only be described as chaotic carnage. The wounded were moaning and screaming while others provided first aid. At the same time there was the ever present possibility of Charlie putting in a counter attack. One of the riflemen from 2 section had taken some shrapnel in the stomach and was screaming for water, which he couldn't have.

"Thank Christ I've been shot in the hip, at least I can drink", thought the section commander, as he gulped down the last of his water.

Nearby, the platoon sergeant was calling in artillery. Flares and tracers lit up the night sky like red rain, while helicopter gun ships provided covering fire, at twelve thousand rounds a minute, while the dust-off helicopters were hovering overhead, winching up the wounded.

Throughout the carnage, the noise and confusion there were selfless acts of bravery and consideration that seems to be the usual thing among front line soldiers. Sharing the last few drops of water, or a cigarette with another, tightening up a bandage for a mate to stop the bleeding.

One of the youngest NCOs, showing real coolness under fire, went out alone into the night dodging Mr. Charles, to look for and guide the reinforcements back. His actions earned him a Distinguished Conduct Medal for bravery.

By now the section commander had lost the capacity for rational thought, with the combination of excruciating pain, shock and loss of blood. Eventually he became semi conscious and thoughts became vacuous, a state in which he could see with unwanted clarity and hear with precision the gunshots. This gave rise to moments of pure calm followed by absolute terror. For some minutes all would seem clear then everything went blurry, he was alternating between the two, when finally it was his turn to be winched up into the helicopter.

He was in the air above the tree line, in a casualty evacuation module, a device which allowed the casualty to be wrapped from head to toe in canvas, with the arms on the outside and a headpiece through which the winch hook could be attached.

To any VC watching, this must have seemed bizarre, a figure like an Egyptian Mummy turning slowly, being winched by the head through the night sky. In his semi-conscious state the section commander had a grandstand view of the surreal spectacle that is jungle warfare at night.

It was like something out of science fiction, watching all this from above with the artillery shells exploding in the distance and the helicopter gun ships flying past, firing continuously to protect him and the other wounded. As he was dragged into the helicopter he saw four others lying on the floor, which was covered with blood. The helicopter crewman was trying to control the situation, looked more like a terrified Martian with his face reflecting the green light from the control panel.

It was like a modern day version of Dante's Inferno.

Within seconds, the flying ambulance was banking away steeply, heading South towards the Australian base, with its' cargo of wounded, moaning and flopping around like dead fish.

As they moved away the section commander saw that the pilots were dressed in black rather than the regulation green, it was a couple of minutes before he realised that in fact the pilots were soaked in sweat, from holding the helicopter at the hover for about fifteen minutes as they winched up the wounded.

They had risked a lot for his section.

Thirty minutes later they landed at the Australian Field Hospital and were met by the triage team, who were trying to deal with more than twenty seriously wounded soldiers. It was absolute mayhem as they sorted them out in order of urgency. The dead, the nearly dead and the living could be considered general categories.

Earlier that day another Australian unit had been involved in a series of mine incidents and there were a number less seriously wounded, still waiting to be treated. Unfortunately, they would be waiting a bit longer, as more urgent cases from the newly arrived wounded were placed ahead of them.

Over the next two days many of these soldiers would undergo multiple operations, the medical teams spending more than 36 hours without sleep and without losing a single patient. Ten days later they were flown back to Australia on a specially equipped Hercules aircraft. As they climbed out over the coast of Vietnam, there was a sense of relief, that they would all make it home alive.

That no one died was due in no small part to the bravery of the dust-off pilots and the extraordinary work done by the doctors and nurses in the field hospital. Of course, most of the wounded would suffer long-term damage but they were alive; and in Vietnam, if you had to come back home before the completion of your tour, the alternative of a plastic bag was not very interesting.

Weeks later, he saw the telegram, sent by the Army, which informed his family that he had been wounded.
"We regret to inform you, that your son is seriously but not very seriously ill, as a result of wounds received in action in Phuoc Tuy Province South Vietnam".

In that moment he realised that while sometimes it may be necessary to take life seriously, it is far too important to be taken very seriously.

AFTER WORD

On the 28th of February 1970, of the 28 soldiers in 3 platoon, A Coy, 6RAR/NZ (ANZAC), fourteen were wounded in action, a casualty rate of exactly fifty percent. This was in addition to nine killed and fifteen wounded by land mines, from 8RAR. In a portent of things to come, Mr. Charles had fought very well. He deserved to win, no maybe about that.

16

ANTS

"The smallest insect can cause death"
Anon

The forward scout moved slowly in the heat of the afternoon sun. He stayed in a low crouch, as he moved under an overhanging branch, trying to avoid the round ball of leaves, which made up the ants nest. He knew from experience, that when the nest was disturbed, the ants would fall by the dozen and attach themselves to any exposed skin, biting ferociously as they hung on until they were slapped off.

"The fucking red ants are everywhere", he thought to himself as he moved on past the ants, pointing out the nest to the others behind him so they could avoid it.

Although the ants were not so much of a distraction for the forward scout, who at that moment amongst all of the Trackers, had what was probably the most dangerous job. Since it was normally the scouts who had first contact with the enemy, more often than not it was Mr. Charles who announced his presence by firing first. The ants were the least of his worries.

In some way the scout could be considered as bait for the enemy, to reveal themselves when they fired at the scout, which would allow the Trackers to move into their contact drill and attack Charlie. The scouts were at both extremes of the military machine, "Expendables who were difficult to replace". No one in his right mind would do that job.

After moving forward another hundred metres past the ant's nest, he saw the edge of a small clearing about thirty metres wide. Normally he would have moved straight across the clearing, but after months in Vietnam, his instincts were razor sharp. He always listened to the primeval instincts of survival, which war brings out in all soldiers.

Often Charlie would take a siesta in the hottest part of the day, between one o'clock and four o'clock in the afternoon. This also gave them the tactical advantage of being still, which made it even more difficult to find Charlie, as opposed to the Australians, who were moving and therefore easier to be seen.

The forward scout stayed in the tree line, even though it would take longer and be more uncomfortable to move around the clearing. From the forward scout's point of view, it was better than cutting straight across, even if there were more ants to be found and the way was harder and longer it didn't matter. The scout had survived eight months and he was determined not to end up as a fond memory for someone else, so early in his life and so close to the finish of his tour.

As he edged around the clearing, he noticed that small shrubs had been cut down, perhaps by nearby villagers or Charlie. Whatever the case he became more focused, more alert as he moved around the clearing. At the same time a couple of hundred metres away, a young Viet Cong had the tedious job of sentry, while the remainder of the patrol he was part of were resting fifty metres behind him.

He sat in a shallow hole watching a line of red ants moving up the rubber tree next to him, flicking one of them away, and watching as it hit the ground. It was a game he liked to play with these insects, which made life miserable for any human they came in contact with. After four months in the Australian sector of Vietnam, he was quite relaxed. He had never seen or heard any Australians and had come to the conclusion that there was no real threat here. Not as it had been further North when he had to deal with large numbers of Americans and Koreans. Yes, he thought to himself, he was quite happy here and continued flicking the ants from the rubber tree. Watching them land about a metre away, smiling as he watched some of them, twitching from side to side.

"There you are you little red shits, how many times you bit me, now you can understand pain and die slowly". He hated them so much that he game left him with a happy smile on his face.

By this time, the Australian scout had nearly completed a half circle to arrive on the other side of the clearing, brushing away a couple of red ants from the back of his neck.

"Jesus fucking Christ! These bastards are everywhere today". He thought shrugging his shoulders. As he tried to understand if the other sensations on his back were due to a combination of heat, sweat and two weeks without a shower or the ants, those "Fucking ants!"

Maybe all that defoliant spray will kill the ants as well as the trees. The scout found that funny, a massive Hercules aircraft spraying defoliant, which had to kill these little red bastards anyway, without the leaves for a nest the ants would be finished. He hated them almost as much as any Viet Cong.

As the Australian scout, followed by the rest of the Trackers circled around the clearing he noticed a couple of footprints made by "Ho Chi Minh Sandals". The footprints could have been one hour or one day old, it was too hard to tell. Now he became much more focused, each footstep taken quietly. All his systems were alert, nostrils flared, mouth half-open, using every sensory nerve possible as if his life depended on it and it did.

The Viet Cong flicked another ant off the tree, when he felt a crawling sensation on the right side of his face beside his ear. Taking his right hand off his rifle, he slapped the side of his face and peeled off a barely moving red ant, shaking it off then scratching his face.

At that moment the Australian scout sensed rather than saw a movement with his peripheral vision and stopped, still, dead still, waiting, peering intently through the low shrubs.

"Maybe nothing", he thought.

The Viet Cong sentry leaned back towards the tree, rubbing his face and started flicking the ants off one by one, his irritation coming close to anger.

By now the scout was about twenty metres away and saw a hand moving down the rubber tree and further down he saw the curved magazine of an AK 47. His left hand gave the thumbs down sign for enemy to the rest of the section behind him.

His right hand bought his M16 to the shoulder and took aim at the Viet Cong. As the scout steadied his rifle with his left hand, the Viet Cong had seen the movement and turned to look at the first and last Australian he would ever see. The VC made a desperate grab for his AK47, when the scout fired a four round burst through his chest, which punched him back against the rubber tree as his rifle spun out of his hands.

As soon as the shots were fired the platoon carried out their contact drill, to secure the surrounding area. With all the shouting and movement from the Australians, the remaining VC understood that there were too many for them to deal with and, as was their usual tactic, ran away to fight another day.

Once the Australians had laid down a defensive perimeter, the scout went across with two of the riflemen to the Viet Cong sentry who was still barely alive. A big piece of his back was missing, the result of four bullets entering his chest at 1,000 metres per second.

"Not much to do", said one of the riflemen, "He's circling the drain". "That was a bloody good shot", said the other rifleman, "How come you saw him?"
"Ah, well he moved", replied the scout.
"Yeah, well that'll do it every time, Jesus, look at those fucking ants, they're on him already", said the rifleman, shaking his head

136

in disbelief, as the ants started crawling over the blood dribbling out of his nose and mouth.

In those last few seconds of his life, as he was loosing consciousness in a haze of pain, the blurring gaze of the young Viet Cong, shifted from the boots of the Australian soldiers to the rubber tree and the last thing he saw, was the column of ants on the rubber tree.

"Those ants, those shitty red ants", he thought, "If they hadn't distracted me, I would have seen him first, fucking ants!"

A few minutes later, after searching the body and finding nothing of value for military intelligence, they buried him in the hole by the rubber tree. As the two riflemen dug the shallow grave, the scout noticed the line of red ants moving up and down the tree and moved his hand across to flick a couple of the ants, then stopped himself.

"That's why I saw him!" he thought to himself, "he was flicking the ants off the tree".

They finished covering the body as one of the riflemen leaned against the rubber tree and flicked a couple of red ants on to the dirt below.

"Come on, let's move down to the others", said the scout, walking away.

17

MILO

Milo had just completed his first year in Vietnam with 4RAR when Bruce "Willy" Williams arrived to take over as Milo's handler.

Willy had nearly two years experience as a dog handler when he arrived in Vietnam. Initially training a young pup called Nero and subsequently with an older dog called Titus, with whom he arrived at 6 Battalion, which was preparing for the next tour of duty in Vietnam.

It wasn't long before they were both well integrated within the tracker teams, as the daily tempo of training increased. Although the Trackers knew that the dogs being used in Australia would not be going to Vietnam, the training was not altered in any way.

A couple of months before departing for Vietnam, while the Battalion was completing the final training exercises, in far North Queensland, Titus died after being bitten by a snake. While all of the Trackers regarded the dogs as part of the team, the relationship between the handler and the dog was always a special one. The handler carried the food, groomed the dog and when they were on training exercises and operations, slept with the dog. Effectively, the handlers and their dogs became a single unit. However unlike the handlers, the dogs seemed to view operational tracking as a game. They obviously could not understand the dangerous nature of the game and that in Vietnam, their lives would depend on each other. As a result when Titus died, Willy was obviously more affected than the others. It didn't matter that Titus wasn't going with the Trackers to Vietnam. For Willy there was a big difference between Titus killed by a snake and leaving him behind, alive in Australia.

There was however a consolation for Willy when he arrived in Vietnam, to find that his new dog would be Milo. A dog he knew from his days at the training centre. It would be Milo with "Willie" Williams and Trajan with "Mooka" Macdonald who would do most of the tracking during the battalion's time in Vietnam.

While we may know, that the difference between humans and animals is that humans can think, there was also a widely held belief among the Trackers, that some dogs had a strong sixth sense. Perhaps this was a result of the combined effects of the dog's strong sense of smell and hearing, whatever the case, some of the tracker dogs seemed to have a stronger "sixth sense" than the others.

When Willy took over as Milo's handler, it was only a few days into the first operation, before Willy noticed the changes in Milo's behaviour, although there was no obvious possibility of a contact, even if he was not following a track, sometimes he became much more alert and intense. He would slow down, sniffing the air, his head moving from one side to the other as if he was searching for Charlie. Within minutes of this change of behaviour there would be signs that Charlie was around.

Certainly all of the tracker dogs had their own personality and Milo was no different. While Trajan was a more serious dog, quieter and more focused, Milo was younger in his behaviour, always ready to play or chase a stick that was thrown for him, or even climb a tree. In fact Milo's favourite item was a beer can, full or empty, through which he developed a definite liking for Fosters beer. This led to Milo being placed on a leash whenever there was a helicopter landing in the vicinity, which required a smoke grenade to be thrown for the landing zone to be identified and since the smoke grenades had a similar shape to a can of beer, Milo would try and run after the smoke grenade. He was always ready to play. Milo's playful nature became an asset when he was on track, full of enthusiasm as he strained on the tracking lead.

On their second operation, a request was made for a tracker team from one of the two New Zealand infantry companies (Victor Company and Whisky Company), attached to the battalion. Milo and Willy were flown in with a small Bell Helicopter to Whisky Company and from the moment that the helicopter landed, Milo was jumping with excitement as the Kiwi patrol commander showed them the start point, which was a patch of blood on the ground, from a wounded VC.

Milo was placed on the track and as usual, Willy started Milo off telling him to, "Seek him! Seek him boy". Milo was at his best when he was playing this game. His tail wagged furiously as he strained on the tracking harness. They had travelled less than two hundred metres when Milo found the scent growing too strong and started to slow down, obviously getting close to the moment when he would point or stop completely.

Suddenly there was a piercing scream from a dense patch of bamboo. It was obvious that the wounded VC was unaware of their presence and just how close he was, to the end of his time on the planet. At that same moment Willy pulled Milo towards him with the tracking lead as he dived onto the ground. Milo could feel Willy's heart pounding as he licked the side of Willy's neck, enjoying the taste of salty sweat, as all dogs do.

In the meantime Willy was indicating the direction of the VC to the Kiwis, as they slowly crept forward. There were a few moments of absolute stillness and silence, perhaps four or five seconds, even Milo had stopped panting, as if he could feel that there was going to be an abrupt end to a life. With a three round burst of fire from one of the Kiwis, the VC was out of his misery.

There was the usual heavy atmosphere, which always existed when someone, friend or foe, was killed or hurt during a contact. After all death by shooting in war, is not exactly a positive moment. Milo was quiet, his exuberant playfulness was missing. It was almost as if Milo, like the other soldiers, was contemplating the enormity of being a participant in the violent death of another human.

It was not until the helicopter dropped them off at the fire support base, that Milo started to regain his exuberance.

Over the next few days and weeks Milo and Willy were sent out on various tracking tasks as a mini team of two with non specialised infantry platoons providing protection for them. With this continuous heavy workload, the days past in a continuous blur, one on top of the other. Most of the days were a combination of absolute exhaustion and total boredom. In fact sometimes it was a relief on those days when Charlie was found or when Charlie found them.

Milo and Willy had been working together for about six months and during that period came to understand each other instinctively. While dogs may not be able to think they can certainly feel. Milo felt the heat, thirst and exhaustion of the dry season along with the foetid stench and humidity of the wet season. He could feel that Willy was tired, whenever the tracking lead would tighten as Willy slowed down as he strained on the tracking lead. In the same way that Willy knew when Milo was feeling the pressure, as the tracking lead would start to slacken when Milo slowed down.

For the dogs and their handlers, the tracking lead became a live action metaphorical umbilical cord. In the same way that mountaineers place their trust in each other on the end of a rope.

As they spent more time together they came to understand the subtle differences in each other's actions. The way Milo slowed down before pointing was very different to the way he slowed down when he was tired.

When Milo was tired his head would drop and move slowly from side to side as opposed to the nose in the air with his ears pricked up as he looked forward with an intense anticipation, slowing down to a very slow walk until he stopped altogether, signifying that Charlie was fifty or sixty metres away.

There was one aspect of Milo's playful nature which was less interesting for Willy and everyone else. This was the occasional lack of focus. The result of this lack of concentration, sometimes found the Trackers spending a long time following the scent of an animal which had crossed the original track. The frustration was palpable, except of course for Milo, who was having a great time. During the dry season Milo and Willy were flown out to D Company to follow up some VC, who had managed to escape from a good sized ambush which had been initiated with Claymore mines. The use of these mines meant that the VC who did not escape were well shredded.

Milo and Willy arrived to find that there were half a dozen dead VC scattered along a well worn track on which the ambush had been set. It was a macabre scene, replete with blood and the broken bodies of young men. The last body was further along the track, draped over the low branch of a tree, about half a metre above the track, with a large section of his skull sheared off, leaving a portion of his brains hanging down onto the track. Milo strained at the leash and started to lick what he no doubt felt was a tasty snack. Not unreasonable from Milo's point of view, particularly since in Vietnam, "Dog" was and still is a favourite "Plat du Jour".

Willy pulled Milo roughly by the back of his neck and shook him saying, "Cut that bloody crap out; behave yourself". For Milo, this was much worse than being hit. When he had done something wrong as a pup, his mother would do exactly the same with her mouth and give him a good shaking. No dog likes a scruff of the neck shaking.

They walked further along the track with Milo suitably subdued until they came up to a clear footprint. As Willy placed him on the tracking lead Milo swiftly reverted to his playful self, for another game. "Seek him boy, seek him", said Willy and Milo was off and running, with nearly all of the twenty foot tracking lead let out.

Most dogs seemed to work better on a long lead even if some handlers preferred using a short lead for easier control. In reality, a distance of an extra ten feet made little or no difference to the outcome. The length of the lead probably depended on a mixture of human psychology and animal instinct, rather than practical application.

From Milo's point of view, it was a game. From Willy's point of view, it really was a life or death situation, Milo's life and his. In effect, the more that Milo enjoyed the game the better he played the game, the better chance they had to win. So, as usual Willy let him run on a long lead.

After about twenty minutes Milo was tracking off to the East or right of the original Northerly direction and the signal was passed along the single file of the infantry platoon, to let them know that there were "Friendlies" on the right hand axis of advance, to avoid a "Friendly Fire" incident, which has never been very friendly.

Over the next hour as they moved through the jungle, Willy noticed that with the change of direction, the track had become much narrower and obscure with virtually no ground sign. As Willy began to doubt the validity of the track, Milo started circling. It was obvious he had lost the track and was moving around looking for the original scent. It was then that Willy noticed the track marks of what appeared to be a wild pig. Obviously, Milo had picked up a fresh animal scent which was more interesting (for Milo) and this new scent deviated away from the original tracking scent of Charlie and his friends.

"What the fuck have you done?" Hissed Willy, in a high pitched whisper. Milo sat with his ears laid back, almost cringing with shame. He knew he should have stayed on the original scent, but the animal scent would have been more interesting for everybody and more fun. From a human point of view Milo had allowed his

144

enthusiasm for the game to overtake rational human thought process. After all how could Milo begin to understand, that his job was to sniff out Charlie for Willy and his friends. Worse than that, they would kill Charlie, when they found him.

Now everyone was pissed off with Milo. The extra hour of tension, as they tracked, during which they expected Charlie to fire on them at any moment. They had done an hour of pointless walking. Make that two hours, because they would have to walk all the way back to the start point. If there is anything Infantry soldiers hate it is to walk for no reason. And all of this for a fucking pig! For the rest of the day, until the helicopter came to pick them up, Milo and in an oblique way Willy, were the focus of everyone's anger, scorn and contempt.

What the others would never understand, is that not all tracks have a successful outcome and that dogs like humans do make mistakes. Perhaps it is the rigid military approach that never allows for failure which breeds this intolerance. Whatever the case, Willy and Milo seemed a rather forlorn team as they waited for the helicopter. Usually other soldiers would come up and pat the dogs or talk to the handler. This time they were left alone.

But they were mates and the essence of mateship is that you stand by them without conditions attached. Milo was unconditional in his loyalty to Willy and in that moment it was the same for Willy.

"Fuckem, they don't even know that Milo is on his second year in this crap hole", he said to himself as he shared his water bottle with Milo, then gave Milo his favourite dog biscuit.

There were many other days of exhausting boredom under tropical downpours or blazing hot sun, depending on the season. There were days of success, failure and sometimes a bit of both. Whatever the day, always at the end, Willy would provide water to drink and a meal for both. In return Milo was always there, the unquestioning loyal mate.

At the end of their time in Vietnam, the Trackers returned to Australia. Of all the days in Vietnam the last day, the day of departure, was for Willy one of the hardest. Full of deep regret, as the army policy of the day, had forced him from a dog handler's point of view, to an act of ultimate betrayal.

He had to leave his mate behind.

Milo stayed on to complete another year with 2RAR followed by yet another year with 4RAR; effectively four consecutive tours of duty. He was the last tracker dog to patrol with the Australian Task Force in Vietnam and completed his last patrol in November of 1971. Shortly after which he was given to the assistant manager of the Chartered Bank in Saigon.

At this point the trail of Milo has no sign left to follow. This would have to be typical of Milo, particularly when I think about those occasions, when Milo would decide to provide us with an unwanted walking tour, as he followed the scent of some animal which distracted him from Charlie. Perhaps he knew that at times it was safer, to follow the ephemeral trail of an animal and avoid taking on Charlie. But that would be a fantasy. While we humans admire others who have that sixth sense or the animal instinct, we know that animals can't think.

A B52 bomb crater makes a perfect pool

18

THE BUSHMAN SCOUT

He would dot and carry one,
Till the longest day was done,
He didn't seem to know the use of fear,
You're a better man than I am Gunga Din.
Rudyard Kipling

A few days after his seventeenth birthday in 1966 Nguyen Xuan Tinh received his notification for military service. He was to report to the headquarters of his provincial cadre a few kilometres from his home.

While his parents were unhappy with his impending departure, they accepted that these were times of sacrifice. Particularly since the Americans had resumed the bombing in the North, which was killing thousands of innocent civilians. Not only that, but every family in the village had been touched by the death or wounding of at least one relative fighting the war in the South. The North Vietnamese and many in the South always saw Vietnam as one country which had been artificially divided by France in 1954 and for them the sense of invasion was real. The South Vietnamese Army was being supported, not only by the Americans but by armies from Thailand, South Korea, the Philippines, Australia and New Zealand.

After more than fifty years of occupation, first by the French then the Japanese, then again by the French, who a decade earlier withdrew after the ignominious defeat at Dien Bien Phu. The idea of yet another foreign power deciding the fate of Vietnam, added insult to injury. This sense of anger permeated all the way to the village where Tinh lived and he, along with the rest of his village, was prepared yet again to fight for their country.

Tinh left home with a sense of anticipation, combined with youthful idealism and invincibility. In the same way as many of those young soldiers, who left home from countries thousands of kilometres away, such as Australia and America.

Over the next six weeks of training he learnt the art of guerrilla warfare, camouflage, concealment and the use of tunnels. How to construct them not only for fighting, but for everyday living. They were built with places to sleep, eat and cook and if necessary fully functional hospitals were built within the system.

When his training was finished, Tinh was sent to a logistics base over the border in Laos, from where he ferried supplies on an overloaded bicycle into South Vietnam. He worked alongside many other young North Vietnamese who were keeping their comrades in the South supplied with the essentials of war. They were among several thousand soldiers, spread out over the "Ho Chi Minh Trail" at any one time during the war. Most of who were pushing bicycles, laden with more than 100 kilos of equipment and ammunition, for their comrades in the South.

In the early years of the war, this route into South Vietnam was the most secure for the North Vietnamese. They needed this to re-supply their troops with food, equipment and reinforcements. Since both Laos and Cambodia were neutral, the NVA were able to avoid the regular bombing carried out along the seventeenth parallel by moving South through Laos and Cambodia.

This situation would change later in the war, as the South and their allies would ignore the supposed neutrality of Laos or Cambodia. Both countries had hundreds of trails going into South Vietnam, many of them able to be used by trucks. However towards the end of the war, in an effort to cut off this logistical support, both Laos and Cambodia would suffer some of the heaviest bombing of the war.

Finally, in December 1967, after nearly eighteen months going backwards and forwards across the border, ferrying supplies to other North Vietnamese units, Tinh's unit was ordered to move into Vietnam. They crossed the border and moved towards the small town of Lao Bao near what was called the DMZ, to wait for further orders.

From the first day in central Vietnam, Tinh saw, heard and felt the presence of the Americans. The sound of their helicopters or low flying forward air controllers during the day seemed continuous and this would be followed at night by the sound of artillery. The most feared were the air strikes by the B52 bombers which would drop sixty 500 pound bombs in one load from a height of six or seven miles. Their approach was never heard and if the bombs landed close by, the ground would shake like an earthquake and anyone directly under the strike had little hope of survival.

The gruelling months ferrying supplies back and forth into Vietnam had taken its toll on Tinh's comrades, several of who succumbed to the effects of malaria and / or dysentery. Although he had lost weight during that time, he was fit enough and ready to fight. They were given a few days so that they could recuperate. During this period they were continually interrupted by the presence of aircraft which had them going in and out of the main tunnel system whenever there was a warning. In the end it was easier for Tinh to spend all day in his allocated space in the tunnel.

After seemingly endless days in the tunnel system, Tinh felt a sense of relief when his company was finally allocated their first operation. They were to provide support for another group who were going to attack an American fire support base. Tinh's company was to move up along one flank of the base and provide covering fire, with RPD light machine guns, as the other groups attacked the base. Prior to this, a group of North Vietnamese sappers would crawl up to the perimeter and try to turn the Claymore Mines around. These mines sat above the ground and contained 750 ball bearings, which exploded outwards at an angle of forty five degrees from the centre of the mine.

If the sappers could turn the mines around without being discovered, when the Americans detonated the mines to defend themselves, they would receive their own ordinance.

In the fading light Tinh and his section moved into position. The attack would start in the early hours of the morning, to give plenty of time for the first group of sappers to deal with the Claymores. As the dawn broke, Tinh was given the order to start firing. Almost immediately, the Claymores were fired by the Americans. The half light of dawn and the flares fired by the Americans illuminated the base. Tinh could see the shadowy figures of his comrades, racing like black ghosts towards the perimeter. They were firing their Kalashnikovs and throwing hand grenades into the shallow bunkers, where the Americans tried to protect themselves.

The second wave followed close behind. Their job was to drag back the dead and wounded. In preparation for this, before the attack commenced, the North Vietnamese had attached two metre lengths of rope to their wrist or waist. The dead and wounded were both treated in the same way. They would be dragged away with the ropes they had attached to themselves for that purpose. If they could walk they would be assisted back to the nearest medical unit for treatment. Often this was part of a tunnel system where the treatment was basic and many of the wounded died as a result of infection.

As the sappers withdrew Tinh commenced firing again. He was full of admiration for those who took part in the assault, wondering how it was possible for anyone to survive the intense machinegun fire from the Americans.

Both sides took many casualties but the Americans would be disillusioned to see only a few of enemy dead, while they had at least thirty five or forty killed in action. Never mind the many more wounded who were waiting for the helicopters to come and pick them up.

In the meantime the Sappers withdrew. They ran back to several designated rendezvous points about five hundred metres away from the American base. Here they had dug and camouflaged several small pits two days previously, as part of the planned assault on the base.

The ones carrying the dead and wounded did not stop, they would continue for several hours before hiding the dead and helping with the wounded. The object of this was frustrate and demoralise the Americans and their allies who placed great importance on the "Body Count". Tinh, like the rest of his unit, found the concept of losing battles but claiming victory by the number of dead bodies laughable.

About fifteen minutes later the helicopter gunships announced their arrival by firing long bursts as they flew along both flanks of the fire support base. The Sappers held their fire, not moving, waiting and watching as they took cover in the small weapon pits.
After two more passes the gunships banked away as the jets came screaming over the tree tops, dropping napalm as close as possible, on each side of the fire support base. For Tinh, this was his first time in action, his first time both figuratively and literally under fire. The aircraft came in one after another in a never-ending series of bombing runs.
"When will this finish?" he thought as the jets let loose another ball of fire.

The heat generated from the napalm was enormous. Tinh knew that the slightest touch of napalm would be agony, since it remained attached to the skin until it was burnt out, resulting in very deep third degree burns. He had heard the stories of others that had died, not from the burns, but from the infection that followed. By this stage he was shaking and wanted to vomit, as he heard two or three moaning in agony, about twenty metres in front of him.

Then, after the fourth bombing run, Tinh had his first understanding of fear as he entered that zone between life and death, the zone of no fear. Where death seemed inevitable and with it the calmness of acceptance.

Suddenly all was quiet, for what seemed like a minute but was only a few seconds and the order was given to advance. In those few seconds, Tinh felt the fear return as he realised that maybe he was not going to die. He had survived his baptism of fire.

His company started moving towards the American base with the acrid small of napalm in the air. Occasionally there was the sickening smell of burning flesh which caught the back of the throat, as they moved passed the charred remains of others who had not been so lucky. It was a smell impossible to forget. The pace picked up as the Sappers started to run forward. They covered each other with a series of leapfrogging runs until they reached the edge of the tree line, as close as possible to the fire support base.

At that moment, two medivac helicopters came arching, over the tree line, banking steeply into the centre of the fire support base. As soon as the helicopters touched down, the Americans carried out their wounded, loading them on as quickly as possible while Tinh and his comrades waited impatiently for the signal to fire. Suddenly one of the rocket launchers was fired at the lead helicopter and everyone started firing at the Americans who were completely exposed. One after another both helicopters exploded, as hundreds of litres of aviation gasoline caught fire, with the wounded still on board.

At this point the Sappers withdrew, disappearing like shadows in the jungle, the only evidence of their attack being five bodies, a few blood trails and the spent cartridges. In the space of two minutes Tinh and his comrades caused enormous damage to the three M's that are pillars of any military operation, Men, Material and above all, Morale.

Although Tinh did not know it, his unit was part of the first of a series of actions which precipitated one of the decisive actions of the war in Vietnam, on a feature which became known as the "Khe Sanh Fire Base". Over the next few weeks this would become the biggest battle of the Vietnam War and the precursor to the TET offensive of 1968.

After the assault, Tinh and his unit made their way towards the Laotian border in a series of forced marches, walking for fifteen or sixteen hours a day. They crossed the border five days later, where they could recuperate and be able to treat their wounded.

Over the next two years Tinh became well versed in the art of jungle warfare and would take part in many similar operations such as the one on "Hamburger Hill". He managed to survive after being wounded on two separate occasions. Quite an achievement since most of the North Vietnamese who were wounded died from post operative infection due to the lack of basic medical facilities.

Eventually, he was promoted to the rank of sergeant major at the age of 20. With his promotion came, orders for him to be posted to Binh Tuy province further south where he would be working with local Viet Cong forces, an area less dangerous than the provinces in the North.

After a series of patrols to recruit men from the villages on the border of Phuoc Tuy province where the Australians were based, Tinh and his unit were taking a well earned rest in one of the large bases run by the North Vietnamese, most of which was underground.

That afternoon Tinh was given the job of securing the perimeter of the base. He had just finished placing the last of his men, when the artillery started to rain down on the base. He knew immediately that one of the Australian patrols had found the base and passed on the coordinates to their artillery. It was only a matter of time before a ground attack would be launched.

Tinh gave the orders for his men to withdraw into the tunnel system, he saw the last of his men nearing the first tunnel when all of a sudden there was a blinding white flash as Tinh was thrown backwards, everything was white, even the trees. When Tinh regained consciousness he felt his whole body vibrating, shaking and realised he was on a helicopter, blindfolded with his hands tied behind him. He could feel some pain in his legs and the effect of the blast, which left him, deafened and concussed.

A few days later he was taken from the American hospital and interrogated for nearly a week, during which he was given a choice. He could change sides and work with the Americans and their allies under the little known Chiu Hoi or Open Arms program. This programme allowed captured North Vietnamese to work with their former enemy, under strict control.

The alternative was, to be handed over to the South Vietnamese who, after torturing him, would place him in their POW camp on Con Son Island. The island was infamous for the so called "Tiger Cages" in which prisoners were left out in the open, no matter what the weather conditions were. The cages were about five feet in length, two feet wide and two feet high. The prisoners would be left in the cages for weeks at a time and fed a bowl of rice, with the occasional piece of chicken once or twice a day. The South Vietnamese guards would entertain themselves by using the cages as toilets, so that the prisoners were continually covered in urine and excrement. The few who survived came out bent and crippled for life, not to mention psychologically destroyed.

For Tinh, if he wanted to survive, there was no option. He chose to join the Chiu Hoi program and become what the Australians called a "Bushman Scout". He was given two months of training where he learnt nothing new, since he had already spent four years countering the tactics he was being taught and in the end, to his surprise, he was sent to work with the Australians in Phuoc Tuy province. He had no idea of what they were like, he had never met anyone who had fought against them but felt that they were probably no different to the Americans.

So it was that in September of 1969 Tinh joined Call Sign 61. The Trackers at the Australian base in Nui Dat and for the eight months that remained before the Trackers returned to Australia, he would work with them and would be one of several Scouts to be integrated into the Battalion through the Tracker Platoon.

The role of the Bushman Scout was to assist in the identification of possible enemy activity, particularly with regard to the signing system used by Charlie, to identify areas that were mined or the proximity of bunker systems.

Once the initial curiosity diminished, most of the platoon accepted the idea of working with a former enemy, although a couple remained sceptical. Meeting Tinh for the first time, two of the NCOs exchanged opinions.

"I mean what the fuck are we doing here? One day we're trying to kill them, next day we're feeding them, Jesus Christ on a crutch!" said one.

"Yeah and if they change sides once, they can change again, fucking great idea, we go in for a section attack with him giving supporting fire, right up our arse, yeah good one," replied the other. While Tinh couldn't understand the words he certainly understood the mood of the two NCOs.

As the weeks past and one operation followed another Tinh became an integral part of the Trackers. With his actions he established a high degree of trust, as the few who doubted him were forced to admit their initial judgement was wrong. His approach was completely fearless, on one occasion when the Viet Cong had fired on the Australians, forcing them to dive for cover, he stood up and deliberately walked towards the VC, calmly firing as he went forward. The Trackers watched, stunned by the bizarre scene of an ex-NVA soldier, fighting against the Viet Cong. Perhaps he knew what the future held and he just didn't care. Whatever his motive, no one could question his courage.

Other North Vietnamese Scouts were assimilated into the Battalion via the Trackers, but for whatever reason, whenever the other scouts were sent to other units, Tinh stayed with the

155

Trackers until their tour was finished. By the time the Trackers were ready to return home, Tinh had made a number of friends amongst them, in particular with one of the Australian forward scouts, Dennis, who with Tinh's help, had learnt to speak some basic Vietnamese.

They had became close friends and on the day that the Trackers left Vietnam, Tinh gave Dennis an embroidered handkerchief showing the map of Vietnam and Australia with two swallows, one flying away towards Australia looking back at the other, still in Vietnam. Unknowingly, Tinh's gift was symbolic of one of the worst betrayals of loyalty by the Australians.

Over the next two years, after the Trackers left, other tracker teams would come and go. They would return to the safety of Australia, while Tinh and the other Bushman Scouts stayed on. In any case there was nowhere else for them to go, they had bet everything, including their lives, that their loyalty would be returned.

One year after the Trackers left Vietnam, while on patrol with the Australians in the Light Green, Tinh was wounded after standing on a land mine. This time his luck had run out. Tinh lost both his legs. Tinh and the other Bushman Scouts, along with the dogs, Marcus, Milo and Trajan were left behind and would have been witnesses as the NVA took over South Vietnam.

The Bushman Scouts would have seen the unforgettable image of the soldier with the North Vietnamese flag, running across the manicured lawn of the United States Embassy, finally placing the flag on top of the American Embassy. An image which reverberated around the world. The Americans and their allies had been defeated, comprehensively.

There is no record of what happened to any of the Bushman Scouts after the Australians left Vietnam. Although it is well known that the NVA did their best to find and kill anyone who had collaborated with their enemies. Certainly the Bushman

Scouts and the tracker dogs deserved better. The only hope one could have, is that if anyone could have survived the programs implemented by the North after their victory, it would have been the brave and ever resourceful Tinh.

19

THE BELLE OF BARIA

*"The smallest love can have the
most serious consequences"*
Fyodor Dostoyevsky

Like many young soldiers, Brian got married a few weeks before leaving for Vietnam. For some it may have been an act born out of the possibility of not returning home, or returning with some body parts missing. Of course, as far as Brian was concerned, that would always be a problem for someone else. He would always make it back home in one piece.

More likely though, as with most marriages of the very young, it was a simple case of emotion overtaking reason. After all, compared to war, deciding to get married could seem a relatively minor matter and easy to do. His wife, Vanessa, considered herself an intellectual, despite failing her first year of an arts degree and dropping out of university. No doubt amongst the ranks of infantry soldiers, few of who had the opportunity of finishing high school let alone a chance of going to university, she could have seemed a mental giant.

Initially, Brian considered himself lucky to have found someone like her, even though she bordered on the obese and at times she seemed a little coarse. He put that down an earthy sense of humour, or perhaps she was just trying to be one of the boys. It was only on the second day of their marriage that his massive error of judgment was underscored. He had been awake for a few minutes when Vanessa rolled over and fired off a flatulent blast of atomic proportions, accompanied by an equivalent asphyxiating stench.

It wasn't so much what she did but rather her subsequent reaction that made him feel uncomfortable and embarrassed. "Pick the bones out of that one!" She exclaimed laughing, without any embarrassment at all.

"Jesus Christ!" Exclaimed Brian, "What are you doing?"

"Well, you're lucky there was no follow through; I could have easily dropped a big brown nugget!" She replied with a smile that showed, not only was there no embarrassment but that she was, in fact proud of herself.

From that day on he saw his wife in a totally different light. How could someone so "sophisticated" behave in that way. Anyone can fart, but not without at least some sense of embarrassment. His respect for her or rather lack of it sank to a new low.

In the remaining weeks, before leaving for Vietnam there were several other instances of the coarsest behaviour. At the same time, there were the continual criticisms of Brian and his friends, along with endless quotes from Plato and Shakespeare. This was done more to show off her "Intellectual Capacity", rather than to underline any part of a discussion. Vanessa continued like this, until those who came to know her often referred to her as "The Educated Idiot". All in all, after three weeks of marriage, Brian was wishing he had never met her.

Departing for Vietnam was a relief for Brian and when he arrived, Brian found that the thousands of kilometres separating him from Vanessa was the ideal distance and from a couple of letters he received from his mates in Townsville, it appeared that Vanessa was enjoying herself on a regular basis in the pubs around town.

It was with this background that Brian went to Vung Tau for his first R and R leave in country. As Brian strolled past the bars he wasn't particularly interested in the women he saw. It was enough to be able to relax, walk around without a weapon and enjoy the occasional beer.

He had been walking through the town for about an hour when he first saw Li Yen, "The Belle of Baria", on a Thursday afternoon standing in front of the "69 Barbers Shop and Steam Bath". It was normally referred to as "The 69" and was not far from the Grand Hotel, which still stands today.

The lithesome Li Yen struck Brian from the first moment he saw her, as she looked at him with a demure half smile. Never mind that she was seated next to the entrance of the best known "Steam and Cream" sauna room in town. Never mind that everyone knew that the girls in The Sixty Nine "worked" and never mind that this was probably one of the busiest short time brothels in the world, where one walked in, paid and got laid. As far as Brian was concerned, she was one of the most beautiful girls he had ever seen in his life.

Li Yen was from Baria, a small village near the Australian base at Nui Dat, but lived and worked in Vung Tau, as a "hostess" in a bar. By the time she was nineteen she had worked for two years at the "Sixty Nine", looking after soldiers from America and Australia. During that time she became an expert in alleviating their sexual frustrations and relieving them of their money in equal measure.

Most young soldiers had the dream of being the hero and of course the unspoken wish to have a girl who would look at his brief life and say, "Wow! you are incredible!" Unfortunately for those soldiers, the women in Vietnam had seen so much of war and the men who fought it that they normally responded with, "You gip me ten dolla, I lup you long time", or "You look so nice, I gip you discaun".

However, sometimes there were those with real class and Li Yen, "The Belle of Baria" was one.
She would stare at the young soldiers with a steady eyed impudence that challenged their naiveté, with an unspoken, "So you want to try me" then she would soften her hard eyes in an

invitation to stay with her. She was after all only a hostess that, "No make other business" until later when there might be discreet negotiations. The best girls could vacuum clean a young soldiers wallet in minutes, while they avoided each others eyes like patrons at a porno movie show, which in fact they were, except for the fact that they were the participants.

The Belle of Baria was good enough to make the soldiers quite comfortable with the rather squalid surroundings; in fact she made them feel happy. Without knowing it, when Brian met "The Belle of Baria", he met one of the best in the business. What should have been a simple commercial transaction rapidly became a passionate love story, at least from Brian's perspective.

The thing was, that Li Yen was so well versed in her trade that she knew exactly how to make the most of every opportunity to relieve soldiers of their money. Unfortunately for Brian, every move she made was in direct proportion to the amount of emotion she could generate which would give a proportionate financial return. She was so good that she could even kiss like a virgin. As the afternoon progressed Brian was gradually drawn into another world by the charms of Li Yen and he made sure, that she could never say that he was a "Cheep Chawee" (Cheap Charlie).

Sure enough, after many expensive Ba Mi Ba beers for Brian and Saigon Teas for Li Yen, with perfect timing, she spoke softly as she ran her tongue around his ear, "Oohh Blian, you no like otha solcha, you look afta Li Yen, you velly nice".
"Oohh, oohh, Li Yen, you so special", replied Brian falling into pigeon English, which after eight years of war had become normal between foreign soldiers and the Vietnamese. He continued:
"Now what do we do?"
"That up to you, depen how much time you hap", replied Li Yen.
"Well, I only have two days, so maybe you like stay with me?"

Brian would discover that there is a bitterness in things too sweet. Like all adventures in love, the beginning is like the smoothest wine one can drink but it is still wine. And too much, almost always leads to irrational behaviour, to be deeply regretted later on.

An hour later they were back at her place, Brian having paid the "bar fine" for taking Li Yen away from her work, before her shift was finished. Minutes after they arrived, Brian leapt on her as if she was the last helicopter out of Saigon, and this was going to be a long flight. After some hours of raw sex, she left him with a sensuous rapture that at times was like an exquisite pain. The afternoon had turned to evening and Li Yen looked after his every whim. Brian was convinced that she was so much more of a "Lady" than Vanessa could ever be.

From his point of view she had the figure of a doll, which was accentuated by the traditional Ao Dai. This consisted of a pair of black pants with a long white dress over the top which was slit on both sides up to the hip, which made her legs seem longer than they were and made her movements seem even more graceful. As the front and back of the dress flowed backwards and forwards whenever she moved. For him she was poetry in motion.

The next two days passed all too quickly for Brian. Li Yen held his hand as they said goodbye and said, "You no wolly, I wait for you come back".
"I send you letter with other soldier when they come Vung Tau", replied Brian, "And I get you good things from American PX store, I look after you". He said as he walked away towards the entrance to the Australian leave centre. By the time he was on the way back to the Australian base at Nui Dat, Brian was besotted with "The Belle of Baria".

From Li Yen's point of view, her manipulations were all related to the practical necessity of survival for herself and her family. Her mother and two younger brothers relied on her financial support ever since the South Vietnamese Army had killed her father two years ago.
Li Yen knew from bitter experience, how fragile life can be in a country at war and that she had only a few years to make the most of her looks. Never mind the fact that since the TET offensive in

163

1968, the North Vietnamese were obviously winning the war and nobody could predict the consequences of that victory. One thing was sure life for a South Vietnamese bar girl would not be pleasant. Li Yen was doing what she could to survive.

The day after Brian returned to Nui Dat he wrote his first letter to Li Yen which would be delivered to her by any one of his mates who would be going on leave to Vung Tau. He couldn't write too often since that would expose a relationship that few soldiers during 1969, in their right mind, would even consider. That is, a serious relationship with a Vietnamese girl. Particularly after months of training in which the Vietnamese were only shown in a derogatory light, with more than a dozen demeaning nick names. Few would be able to deal with the derision that would come with "falling in love", with a "Nog". Brian knew he would be the laughing stock of many in the platoon if they ever found out. He never told anyone, covering his letters with, "Yeah, it's just to make sure, you know for a good R and R. Root and Rave, that's what it's about". He would say with an awkward laugh.

Seeking solace in the arms of a prostitute was not unreasonable under the circumstances. A twenty-year-old soldier desperate for a girl, with a marriage that was so short, there was barely time to unwrap the presents before it was over. All of this and a war to fight would overwhelm anyone, let alone a naïve young soldier away from his country for the first time.

The next operation was a welcome distraction for Brian; he couldn't stop thinking about Li Yen. There were some days when he would volunteer for extra patrols to try and put her out of his mind but try as he might; she was there in his minds eye. Sometimes he would have imaginary conversations with her, especially at night when he was alone in his thoughts.

The weeks dragged on slowly, until finally, after two months the next allocation of Rest and Recreation leave came due. Within an hour of arriving in Vung Tau, Brian was on his way to "The 69". As he came around the corner he saw her sitting there, just as she was the first day that he met her. She gave him her professional smile, designed to make him think he was the only person in the world for her.

"Oh Blian, you come back, I know you come back, I so happy", said Li Yen as she took his arm with both hands and led him inside.
"You like same same as before, very nice" replied Brian using the standard form of pigeon English.

Over the next three days Li Yen came to know all of Brian's secrets and problems. Of course, Brian thought that he knew all of Li Yen's secrets. In fact nobody really knew anything about "The Belle of Baria". Like so many in a one-sided romance, he had unknowingly created an exotic and elaborate figment of his imagination. Of course, amongst all the soldiers that Li Yen had serviced, she had processed at least half a dozen like Brian. She saw them as bonuses to be milked for all they were worth. She initiated the next step by planting the seed in Brian's mind, while they were having lunch, by saying.
"I sad that you alledy mallied Blian, if you not then.." she left the sentence unfinished.
After a few seconds silence, Brian said, "Well I am going to get divorced when I go back".
"What you mean divorced?" asked Li Yen, knowing full well what it meant.
"Means I not married anymore", replied Brian.
"Other girls tell me same happen to them but soldiers go back home and no see again", said Li Yen, looking sadly at her hands fiddling with a table napkin.

"But it true, I tell you before about my wife" said Brian in a hurt tone.

165

"Yes, I know you good man Blian but what you can do?" She asked, and then continued without waiting for a reply, "Maybe Buddhist wedding can do".

"What you mean Buddhist wedding?" He asked.

Li Yen then gave him a short explanation of a Buddhist wedding ceremony, which Brian had heard something about before.

From Li Yen's explanation, he understood that it was a brief ceremony presided over by a Buddhist monk which required a witness from each person and could be organized in a couple of days.

"Look", said Brian, "Maybe we can make ceremony next time I come Vung Tau, what you think?" asked Brian.

"Oh you do this Blian, leally? Maybe you jus say words", she replied.

"No, we can do this, sure", said Brian.

They spent the rest of the afternoon planning, how they would do this on Brian's next leave in Vung Tau. Of course there were going to be expenses for the monastery, the monk, Li Yen's family would come down from Baria and, of course, there would be the party and the gifts which tradition required that the bride and her family should receive with no expense spared. Brian was aware that this was going to be quite an expensive undertaking. He knew that Li Yen was doing her best to avoid spending too much. At least he thought so. In fact, Li Yen knew how to play the game. After all this was her third "Wedding" and she was able to skim nearly half of all the money for herself and her family. She was a survivor, nothing personal in any of this. She would do whatever it took to survive.

They went to the Buddhist monastery on the hill which overlooked the town of Vung Tau and met the monk who would conduct their ceremony and the three of them had their photo taken at the front of the monastery. For Brian there was a sense of

166

the unreal, after all he could never have expected that his life would take this course.

The morning before Brian left for the Australian base, he withdrew one thousand dollars from the paymaster's office, which represented the last three months pay. When he gave Li Yen the money she was obviously pleased with her effort but at the same time a little surprised, that Brian was so obviously in love with her. After they said goodbye, Li Yen thought there could be a possibility she could get out of Vietnam. Maybe he was serious and not like the others, who made promises that were always broken when their twelve months in Vietnam was over.

At the Australian base, the operational cycle continued as Brian's company was preparing for the next operation. He packed his gear automatically; his mind totally distracted by thoughts of Li Yen.

Brian had written to Vanessa, taking some satisfaction in letting her know that not only would he be divorcing her when he returned but that from now on the only money she would receive from his pay would be the allowances she was entitled to and nothing more. Two days later the next operation started in an area called the "Light Green" located near a group of hills called the Long Hais. This was an area notorious for land mines and responsible for more than thirty percent of all Australian casualties. They had been patrolling for nearly two weeks and the strain of operating with the continuous threat of land mines was beginning to show, with two extreme forms of behaviour. The soldiers were either totally focused, with a lot of tension on full alert or they just didn't care. Brian's attitude was in the latter category, not because he didn't care but because he was continually distracted by thoughts of Li Yen and his new future with all the possibilities and problems that would bring, above all the fact that in a few days he would be seeing Li Yen again. His company would have three days in Vung Tau ahead of schedule, as their next operation would be extended to six weeks.

167

A couple of days previously, Brian had approached his best mate, Davo, to ask him about being a witness at his "Wedding". Davo had heard of others doing this so that they could have "Permanent Bang" available during the tour of duty. So he was quite surprised, when he realized that Brian was seriously in love with a Vietnamese bar girl. In spite of his reservations, he didn't criticize Brian and agreed to be a witness and not say anything to the others. After all he was a mate. It was late in the afternoon on day fourteen of the operation Davo was following about eight metres behind Brian. He could see that Brian was switched off, "Quite logical", thought Davo, with all of this in going through his mind Brian would be totally distracted. At this point the Vietnamese Bushman Scout signalled that there was something suspicious up front. A few minutes later a Mini Team of two combat engineers who specialized in mine clearing were called forward to check for mines since the Bushman Scout had seen what he thought was a sign beside the track which indicated a mine or a booby trap further forward.

The infantry soldiers were more than happy to take a break from patrolling while the Engineers went forward to make a clear lane with their mine detectors. It took the Engineers an hour to clear a lane, which they marked with white tape on each side, the area between the tapes being the safe lane. Once the Engineers returned to the rear of the patrol, they started moving forward again.

By now the last thing that Brian could concentrate on was patrolling through the low scrub and sand of "The Light Green". Under the hot tropical sun, tired and thirsty, with his pack cutting into his shoulders, he was looking forwarding stopping for the day. Just to stop and rest. The best he could do was to put foot in front of the other. While he thought about Li Yen he started another imaginary conversation with her, looking down at the barrel of his rifle.

Suddenly as Brian placed his left foot down, he saw the white tape under the barrel of his rifle. "Oh shit! I've crossed the tape!" he thought to himself.

At the same time he heard Davo yell, "No Brian!"

His foot had barely touched the ground when he felt rather than heard the "click", in almost the same moment followed by a loud bang and a burning sensation on his back and his legs as he was flung through the air. The next thing he was aware of was a lot of shouting and yelling. He could move his legs and had no pain, but even as he moved his legs his body wouldn't move.

"Davo! Davo! Where are you?" He yelled. There was no answer. Davo was killed the instant the mine exploded seven or eight metres in front of him. The combination of blast and shrapnel left him in pieces. Brian was dazed and going into shock when the medic finally got to him. "Don't worry you'll be all right, the dustoff is on the way", said the medic as he applied a tourniquet above the knees of both legs.

"What happened? My left leg really hurts", said Brian.

"You'll be ok. You'll be going home", replied the medic. This was definitely not the moment to tell Brian, that his left leg was virtually non-existent and the right leg below the knee looked about the same.

After what seemed forever, the dustoff helicopter arrived and they carried Brian through the safety zone marked by the white tapes. He could see the small hole on the left of the tape, outside the safe zone. A short distance away he could see a bloodied body with an arm missing, not moving. There was a sweat rag wrapped around the head, just as Davo used to do. Beyond that there were at least half a dozen other wounded who were moaning and asking for water. Even though he was in shock, Brian knew that his lack of concentration was responsible for the carnage in front of him.

Then came a moment of harsh reality, "What about Li Yen?" he thought. "Oh No!" Everything came flooding through. As

Brian passed out, he realized that in a split second his life had been changed, changed forever. It was on his third day in hospital that Brian was able to think a little more clearly through the mist of morphine. He could see tubes running into each arm and another lower down under the blanket.

"How are you feeling Brian?" asked the nurse.
"I've got cramps in my back and legs, I can't move, I am so sore umm, my left knee, my left knee is really sore, I think I really fucked up, umm", he trailed off without finishing the sentence and started sobbing as the combination of pain and the realization of what he had done started to sink in.

"Ok, Brian we are going to put a ripple mattress underneath you with water in it that is moved by a pump, so you won't have anymore cramps. Then I'm going to give you something to help you sleep and take away the pain", said the nurse as she checked the tube running into his arm. Brian could only nod his head.
    It was another two days before Brian began to understand what happened. He was helped into a sitting position by two medics who had come to wash him.

"Jesus my left knee hurts", said Brian.
The medics said nothing as Brian looked down along the bed, realizing with horror that his left leg didn't exist. In surgical terminology he had undergone, a Hindquarter, which effectively amputates the leg all the way down from the hip. That was not all, as he lifted the sheet to look at what had been done, he saw that his right leg had been amputated just above the knee. Brian was numb with shock. One of the medics put his hand on his shoulder and said, "Look mate, it is bad, but not as bad you think. There is a lot they can do, the surgeon will let you know what your options are but we have seen worse here, like you wouldn't believe".
Brian was crying, silently.

When the medics left, he started to replay in his mind what had happened, something he would do over and over again for the rest of his life. Trying to understand how he could have been so stupid.

Nobody went outside the white tapes, just as nobody crossed the white lines on the road. Well, people did cross the white line when they were distracted and they had accidents. Strange thought Brian in a more lucid moment. The colour white is so significant in life and death. Vanessa wore a white wedding dress, not that she was a virgin. Babies are christened in white, white lilies are used for funerals.

In war white is the colour for surrender. The Sikh warriors wore white under their uniforms, to be ready for death. Moslems wrap their dead in white. The idea of white as the colour for mine marking, to indicate the line between life and death in a minefield seemed quite appropriate under the circumstances.

What about Davo his best friend? The memory would stay with Brian until the day he died. Davo's head, mashed in from the blast, unrecognizable with his arm detached from his body. Davo caught the full blast.

The guilt that hung over him was made worse, when he looked across the ward and could see "Thomo" and "Dutchy", two riflemen from his platoon. Both of them had taken shrapnel in the face and chest, which would leave them disfigured for life.

Through all this, Li Yen would enter his thoughts, adding to the emotional chaos. What a disaster, what a mess. No Li Yen, no wife, Davo gone, the rest of his mates wounded and worst of all, twenty years old and no legs. His life destroyed in an instant, through his own stupidity.

Later that morning, the surgeon came and spoke with Brian, explaining what had been done and how the amputation of a limb or limbs affects people in different ways. How the emotional loss could be like losing a relative and it would take time to adapt to

171

such a loss. Physically his body would be permanently altered and this would affect all areas of his life. How much his amputation affected his life would, to some degree depend on the extent of his physical recovery. Before Brian could ask, the surgeon said, "Regaining the ability to walk would be a major achievement".

This was the kindest way to say that in Brian's case, as a double amputee with a hindquarter amputation, he would be in a wheel chair for the rest of his life. The surgeon then continued with what the next few weeks held in store for him.

During the recovery period, pressure sores could develop due to lack of mobility and there was always the possibility of infection around the stump, which could mean revising the amputation (code for removing more of the leg). There was no need to explain phantom limb pain, since Brian had already experienced it in the last two days, from the now non-existent right knee. The surgeon finished by placing his hand on Brian's shoulder and saying, "Don't worry, you'll be home soon and things will seem much better then". Brian was dumbfounded.

There was the fact that he was now a cripple, he would never walk again. Then there was Li Yen. He didn't want to go home, he wanted his legs back, and he wanted to see Li Yen.

He didn't care about going home. Over the next few days Brian wallowed in deep depression, until the day came to leave Vietnam.

A special medivac Hercules aircraft was used, with three layers of stretchers between the floor and top of the cabin; these ran down the centre of the aircraft. The plane had a full load of broken bodies to be repaired when they arrived back in Australia.

For Brian, the emotions became more acute, so he exaggerated his pain, just to get another shot of morphine to kill the emotion. From his position on the top stretcher, through the window, he could see the town of Vung Tau as they turned eastwards towards Australia and through the thick mist of his tears, came the apparition of Li Yen, "The Belle of Baria", just as she was on the first day they met, with that demure smile.

In the meantime Li Yen reserved some space in her mind and in her schedule for the young Australian soldier. Knowing he should be there for the "wedding" on the 24th of July. If the Australian soldier really did work out, that would be a dream come true. Not because she loved him, just that she could survive with a chance to be out of Vietnam.

By the 26th of July, Li Yen understood that Brian would not be coming to see her; he was just another one who said the words. She should have charged him the same as her other clients. A few days later, as the "Belle of Baria" was sitting in front of the 69 Bar, she watched as a large aircraft climbing out over Vung Tau and then turn steeply to the East. She could see the red kangaroo painted on the side and her face hardened.

"Uc Da Loi Cheap Charlie, same same like other soldiers", she thought to herself, as her face became a year older and a year harder. One needed to be hard, very hard, to survive in her line of work.

When Brian arrived home he went through a series of secondary operations followed by physiotherapy, spending nearly two months at the repatriation or veteran's hospital in Melbourne.
Vanessa came to see him twice in hospital, the second time with the documents to be signed to commence the divorce proceedings. She had found someone else. In fact she had found "someone else" a couple of months after Brian had gone to Vietnam.

The months went by as Brian adapted to a bitter life without legs and without independence, which often meant relying on others for mobility. In 1970 there were few places with access for wheel chairs. Even the hospital had only one entrance with wheel chair access. Brian also found that people would talk to him more

173

readily; sometimes it may have been out of pity or perhaps because they felt less vulnerable, or maybe because they knew that he could not just walk away. In any case, people just seemed to find it easier to talk to someone in a wheel chair.

At times people would ask the most bizarre questions in the most patronizing way. One woman asked him at a veteran's function, "And tell me, what is the most difficult aspect of your condition"?

To which Brian replied, "Well, have you ever tried wiping your arse without your feet on the ground?" The startled look on the woman's face was enough to make him continue with, "Don't worry, I'm used to the skid marks on the undies". He said with grim satisfaction as the woman scuttled away to find someone more amiable.

Every day Brian would be confronted with the biggest mistake of his life or at least the result of it in the morning when he dragged himself out of bed or when he had a shower, when he needed to use the toilet, especially a public one. Although he solved the latter by taking a large thermos flask with him when he went out for a few drinks. It had a wide opening in which he could pee without leaving the bar.

Brian could walk on artificial legs but only with crutches. The surgeon was right when he said walking would be a "Major Achievement". It was impossible. The consequence of a hindquarter amputation in a double amputee was total instability of the prosthesis and continual breakdown of skin tissue at the point of contact with the prosthesis.

Nearly five years later, Brian watched the news, as the American helicopters took the last of the Embassy staff from the roof. Charlie had achieved the impossible; against tons of bombs, artillery, napalm and the most advanced technology of the day, Charlie had won. As he watched the scene on TV he thought about Li Yen, as he had done every day since they met. "I wonder what she is doing, what happened to her?"

174

Brian had read about re-education camps that were to be set up for "collaborators" and hoped that Li Yen would avoid that prospect. In any case, while Brian did think a lot about Li Yen, he found himself more frequently thinking about his next bottle of beer, bourbon or Black Label whiskey.

By 1980 Brian had made a conscious decision to turn his wheel chair around and look forward to the past. The future was too difficult to contemplate; it was one without hope. The years passed and Brian found himself immersed in an alcoholic haze with his mates in the pub. As he often said, "Much better a bottle in front of me than a frontal lobotomy". Life was easier like this.

Eventually, he moved to a small country town where he rented a two-bedroom house, equidistant between the only two pubs in town. Where, after paying the rent and electricity with his pension, he had plenty left over to become the best customer of both pubs. Every evening, his wheel chair could be seen on the veranda of one pub or the other, from lunchtime to sunset and occasionally before. After which, he would buy a bottle of whiskey or wine and manoeuvre his wheel chair some five hundred metres back home.

Sometimes, if he had spent the whole day at the pub, his wheel chair would take a circuitous route back home. Moving along the edge of the road, crossing and re-crossing the white line on the side of the road. In the process he would be cursing and swearing in a mantra like fashion, "Fucking mines, fucking white lines; fucking mines, fucking white lines". Occasionally people would see him and hear his personal mantra, as he made his way back home. They put it down to a simple matter of another "Vietnam Vet" who had lost the plot.

It went like this for some years until in 1989 on a July afternoon, exactly twenty years after having his legs blown away, Brian hadn't been seen for at least a week. A couple of old regulars from the pub went to his house. The door wasn't locked and after calling out his name with no reply, they went inside.

Inside the atmosphere was squalid and dirty, with empty bottles of wine and whiskey scattered throughout the house. Dirty plates in the kitchen, unwashed clothes in the bedroom, nothing had been cleaned for weeks.

Brian was nowhere to be seen, until they went to the back of the house, where the second bedroom was located. Here, there was a very different scene. The floorboards polished, the walls sparkling white, with a Buddha statue in the far corner and some burnt out incense sticks at the feet of the Buddha. Beside the Buddha, was Brian in his wheelchair, one of the men tried to move him but rigor mortice had set in and he was obviously dead.

Perhaps it was a deliberate decision or an accidental overdose, either way, twenty years of alcohol, antidepressants and painkillers achieved what the landmines couldn't. He seemed to be asleep, his head to one side with a slight smile on his face, finally at peace with the world.

Clasped in his hands was a silver frame with an old black and white photo, of a young Australian soldier with a Vietnamese girl in a white Ao Dai and a Buddhist monk standing in front of a monastery.

20

HELICOPTERS

The definitive icon of the war in Vietnam is probably the Bell HU-1 Iroquois helicopter, nicknamed "Huey". Although later on the US Army changed the designation HU-1 to UH-1 (Utility Helicopter), the name Huey stuck. Every infantry soldier knew Huey well.

There was never any mistaking their characteristic wop-wop-wop sound, caused by the huge fifteen metre tip to tip rotor blades with a width of half a metre. There was always a sense of relief when we heard "Huey", it meant that we didn't have to walk.

It was only decades later, when I sat behind the controls and flew a small Lynx helicopter with an instructor, that I was able to appreciate the complexities of flying one.

There are three basic control systems; the collective and the cyclic which are like two sticks and the "rudder pedals" on the floor.

The collective is located on the left side of the pilot's seat. Lifting the collective increases the pitch of the main rotor, causing the helicopter to rise and lowering the collective will decrease the pitch of the main rotor, causing the helicopter to descend. There is a throttle twist grip at the end of the collective stick which has to be coordinated with the up and down movements in such a way that more throttle must be twisted in as the collective is raised and the throttle rolled off as the collective is lowered.

The cyclic control stick rises vertically from the cockpit floor between the pilot's legs. Moving the cyclic stick in any horizontal direction will cause the helicopter to move in the direction that the cyclic is pushed.

The "rudder pedals" are effectively tail rotor control pedals which when applied change the pitch of the tail rotor, so that when the left or right pedals are pushed the nose of the helicopter will move in the direction of the pedal that is pushed.

Armed with this knowledge and the fact that I had held a licence to fly fixed wing aircraft, gave me the misguided fantasy that flying a helicopter would be easy enough to learn.

I arrived half an hour early, full of anticipation, for my first lesson at the Helicopter Training School in Melbourne. After a ground briefing of about 45 minutes, we walked out to the small two seater Lynx helicopter. It was nothing like the Huey in size or complexity, but at least a taste of what flying a helicopter would be like.

My instructor Damien was about twenty years old and made me feel positively ancient as we walked around the helicopter, doing the pre-take off check after which we climbed into the machine and ran through the start up and internal checks. He had all the confidence that comes with many hours of flying and youthful surety.

The main rotor turned faster and faster until we were at steady roar as we started to take-off. There was a slight lurch upwards and forwards and we were in the air.

I was overwhelmed by the noise, vibrations and the way all the instruments seemed to have a life of their own. The vibration seemed to make the instruments blurry and unreadable. So unreadable, that at one stage, I thought we were flying at the impossible speed of three hundred knots an hour!

This was nothing like flying a fixed wing aircraft.

We were about ten minutes flying time from the training area and I used those minutes to try and orientate myself and to understand the location of the instruments. I had located the altimeter,

178

compass and airspeed indicator when Damien said, "OK, Percy, you have the collective and all you have to do is keep us at the same height and airspeed".

I held the collective with my left hand trying to cement both my hand and the collective in exactly the same position, so we would maintain the same height and airspeed.

"No need for white knuckle flying here", said Damien, with a smile, "Just relax and if you need to adjust try and feel it with your fingers".

After a couple of minutes I thought I was going reasonably well when Damien said, "Not bad, now you have the cyclic, so just keep us headed in the direction at this height and airspeed".

"I have the collective and the cyclic", I replied with a little more confidence. Within less than a minute, I was flying 200 feet higher and oscillating 20 degrees either side of the original course as I continually over corrected.

"My aircraft", said Damien

"Your aircraft", I replied, trying not to sound too disappointed.

"Right", said Damien, "We'll start again".

And so it went on for about half an hour until I could hold a course and altitude within what Damien considered reasonable boundaries for a student pilot. As I tried to maintain direction and height I must have been at the limit of those boundaries, oscillating from one over correction to another.

Eventually we arrived back at the airport hovering about twenty feet above the ground, near the helicopter landing area, when Damien said, "Now we are going to try the last part of the introductory flight. You see that small building in front of us?".

I nodded.

"Well, now you will have all three controls, I want you to keep us in the same place, same height and with the foot pedals keep us lined up with the building, ok?"

"Understood", I said.

"Your aircraft", said Damien.

"My aircraft", I replied and promptly had us pointing some 60 degrees away from the building.

"Shit!" I said, as I over corrected and had us facing 60 degrees in the other direction.

Damien said, "Just slow down, relax and try to make small corrections, particularly with our altitude", he added ironically, "Since there is no underground car park here".

It would need many more hours of training before I would be able to handle the basics of helicopter flying.

If this explanation of an instructional flight along with the practical application of the basic control systems is complex, consider how much more difficult this becomes when there are more than ten other control functions such as, external and internal radio communications, landing light switch, winch release switch, machine gun trigger, all of which are located on the collective and the cyclic control columns.

Within all of these functions, there was also the issue of navigation, in an era when there was no such thing as a GPS and which was always made more difficult during the wet season.

While the Huey had a pilot and co-pilot to share all of these tasks, there was an enormous amount of pressure on both of them since war time flying in tropical Vietnam came with some unique problems.

The first and obvious one was the load factor or "Overload Factor" would be a more apt description. While the Huey was certainly capable of flying with a section of ten infantry soldiers, two crew and two pilots under normal conditions. The wet season with its hot humid air, meant that there was much less lift available, making the machine overloaded and unable to take off normally.

There were however two techniques which were used frequently in Vietnam.

The first was to kick one of the soldiers off the Huey and put him on a later flight. For obvious reasons, this could only be used at the Nui Dat base camp, since abandoning a soldier in the bush was not an option.

The other option entailed picking the machine up to a hover, then accelerating in a circle flying close to the ground, until the helicopter achieved "transitional lift speed".

That was the moment at which we always felt a sense of mild exhilaration with the sudden rise in the helicopter's speed and height. I always thought it was part of the adrenaline of a helicopter pick up and it wasn't until much later, that I understood it was a necessity. One that required skilful flying under difficult conditions, with the potential danger that is associated with flying overloaded, using the physics of transitional lift.

Often we would see the pilots put down into impossibly small clearings, with very low visibility. Sometimes they would use the strength and inertia of the 48 foot blades with ballast weights at each blade tip, to chop through small branches to drop off a patrol. Occasionally large branches were hit and the rotor blades would have to be replaced, at the equivalent cost of over $100,000.00 in today's dollars.

The Huey had another characteristic which the pilots called the "Huey Tuck". On take-off, if the landing zone was large enough, the pilot would lower nose over as it gained airspeed. However, if it was nosed over too far, the wind resistance on top the flat roof would force the nose over even lower. The machine would then try to dive into the ground as it accelerated.

If this happened over level ground then a vicious circle would be created. Pulling back on the cyclic to lift the nose would not overcome the pressure on the roof. Pulling up on the collective to stay away from the ground only added more power, causing a crash at an even higher speed. If nothing was done there would still be a crash, just at a lower speed.

The skills and multi-tasking required by the pilots to fly the Huey in Vietnam, were exceptional, particularly when they came under fire on a patrol insertion or extraction.

Apart from actually flying the Huey and navigating to drop off a patrol at the right place, there was also the continual radio "chatter" between the pilots and the crew, other aircraft nearby and their own base.

As one of the pilots said to me years later, "When all this is combined with some skinny little guy on the ground firing his machine gun at you, the exercise can become very confusing, particularly when the helicopter is hit and you have an emergency to deal with.

Of the many unforgettable moments in terms of flying skill and courage, that Huey provided us with, one of the most memorable was the evacuation of seven sick and wounded prisoners of war, which we had captured in the May Tao Mountains.

The terrain was very steep with a lot of trees. After a lot of searching and discussion by radio with the pilots, it was decided to use a large rock on a steep spur line. The rock shelf had prevented the growth of vegetation, in particular tall trees that covered the mountain. This gave the effect of a small clearing, enough to allow a Huey to enter. Although it could not land the Huey could be flown in and one skid placed on the rock. So that while the pilots could keep the helicopter balanced, one skid in the air and one on the rock, the trackers would lift up the sick and wounded enemy on to the rock and load them into the helicopter.

The level of flying skill to maintain this position was exceptional, since as each POW was loaded on board the helicopter would lurch from side to side and the pilots had to maintain a level platform. Any radical shift would have resulted in the helicopter blades striking the ground on the upper slope of the hill, with disastrous consequences.

At the same time there was still the issue of Charlie whose major centre of residence was in the May Tao Mountains. Everyone was aware of the irony in this situation. Especially the pilots, who were placing all their skills and taking a big risk for the lives of some seriously wounded enemy.

While the pilots were dealing with this rapidly changing situation, there was the continual background radio chatter on their own radio net which controlled their mission, the door gunners and of course us on the ground.

Eventually the task was completed in two separate flights, both of which, from an infantryman's point of view, were both skilful and enthralling. Everyone watched what could only be described as "Trick Flying", never seen before or since, as Huey wobbled precariously with each wounded loaded on board. The only word to describe the capacity of the Huey and the pilots for this type of flying was, "Extraordinary".

During that long war in Vietnam, Huey flew more than fifteen million sorties in combat assaults, medivac, re-supplies of food and ammunition.

Huey and the pilots have been referred to as "God's Lunatics" Even when the situation was bleak and there was no way out, there was always Huey.

One night, near the end of our time in Vietnam with fourteen wounded and Charlie making life very difficult for us, we heard that signature beat of the rotors and knew that the ever reliable Huey had come to save us. They couldn't land, so they stayed at the hover and lowered the winch cable some sixty feet, to lift up the wounded.

They stayed until they had winched up all the wounded, hovering for fifteen or twenty minutes at a time, in spite of the fact that they were a perfect target, they stayed, rock steady.

They might have been known as God's Lunatics, but when they came to pick us up they were God's Angels

Today when a plane or a helicopter fly's overhead, people often look up with a brief glance.

183

However when a Huey fly's past, there is the occasional one in the crowd who will stop and gaze intently until the faint wop wop wop of the blades are no longer heard, with a nostalgic look on their face and a fond remembrance the pilots and crews of that extraordinary machine; Huey.

She was always there when she was needed.

21

FROM THE DIARIES
"We are what we remember".

Most of us have rather unstable memories. A diary however tends to give a different reality to the memory and while the writings now seem juvenile, they were after all written by a young and naïve nineteen year old soldier.

They were notes written in real time or at least shortly afterwards. So they are not obscured by the mists of time, although one is still mildly surprised to be taken aback (in retrospect) by situations that were after all quite normal, in the business of humans behaving badly and killing each other. In some of the anecdotes I have added to or taken away some of the notes if I felt there was too much opinion or that it could be too offensive. As usual there was always irony and black humour, in abundance.

THE DIARY – 1967

"The Sergeant had florid features, a face which had a light red hue that seemed to blaze along with the sun, becoming more red after lunch. Of course that was in keeping with his the nature of his work and his recently completed second tour of Vietnam. The fact that he was an alcoholic probably helped"
Recruit Training May 1967

THE DIARY – 1968

"Beware of pretty girls who may be spies as well as bicycles, revolvers, arms dead horses and men lying on roads. They are not there accidentally".
Soviet Army Training Manual 1938

Watch careless talk about your unit and operations and innocent conversations; for instance women are often used to getting information from soldiers on leave. At this time you become vulnerable, to physical terrorist attacks from such things as bicycle mines and grenades"
Australian Army Training Manual 1968

"It became necessary to destroy the town to save it".
US military briefing officer, after the destruction of the provincial town of Ben Tre during the Tet offensive of 1968.

"We have to consider the possibility that we will lose"
US military briefing officer one day after the Tet offensive of 1968.

"There will be no more press briefings by field officers. In future all briefings will be through the Military Command Office in Saigon".
Order from MACV two days after the Tet offensive of 1968

"Fresh Vietnamese Meat – 300 piastres a pound".
A sign placed on four North Vietnamese corpses Tet 1968.

THE DIARY – 1969

SIGNS AND PHRASES
Helmets and Hats;
For many Australians and Americans, writing on a bush hat or helmet was a form of individuality, a way to express separation from the "Green Machine", a silent expression of mutinous thought, which was taken on by many. For others it was an affirmation of a just cause.

I-H-T-F-P .... I hate this fucking place.

"Our bisness (sic) is killing and bisness (sic) is good"

The peace sign with "War Sucks" written underneath.

"Fighting for peace is like fucking for virginity"

Amongst black Americans "No VC ever called me Nigger", was popular.

Of course there were other more jingoistic American phrases.
"Kill a Commie for Mommie"

"We kill for peace".
The unofficial motto of some American special forces.

A rattle snake with "Don't tread on me" written underneath.

"Only You Can Prevent Forests"
Proudly displayed by the pilots who flew the Agent Orange missions known as "Operation Ranch Hand".

"Who Cares Who Wins".
Towards the end of the war, even the SAS were rather jaded and while this was never written it was occasionally said, as a twist on their own motto of "Who Dares Wins".

MAY 1969
"Vietnam—Life is not for everyone.... just remember, we are all in this alone!"
May 1969; note left on a table for new replacements.

ON A NEW CIGARETTE LIGHTER
"Yea though I walk through the valley of the shadow of death I shall fear no evil.... For I am the evilest son of a bitch in the

187

valley". An alternative version of "The 23rd Psalm" engraved on the standard "Zippo" cigarette lighter. One of the "Must Haves" for the infantry soldier, but more often than not found in the possession of rear echelon clerks. After all, Vietnam did little to make infantry an attractive proposition.

JUNE 1969
THE BATTLE FOR BINH BA
"The North Vietnamese came and after killing whoever was there, took anything of value, burned the huts and then they left"
Bin Bah after action report.

"They came, they sacked, they burned, then they were gone."
Henry Yule on the Mongols 11th. Century sacking of Bokhara.

RADIO TRANSMISSION
"Red Eagle Two Fahve this is Pit Bull Nayn Sehven…. Man you puttin rounds inta ma backyard. You keep doin that ah ain gonna have no backyarrd no more…ya hear"

"This is Read Eagle Two Fahve…..Real sahrry…you got any idea where ah can drop the rest of ma shit?"

"This is Pit Bull Sehven….Ah don know… jus stop fuckin up ma backyard!"
Radio transmission, between an American fire support base and a forward air controller. June 1969.

A MATE

Have you ever been tired?
Not the everyday tiredness, but the absolute exhaustion that leaves you desperate for the rest you can't have. That feeling when time seems to stretch on to infinity. That this could go on forever.
Maybe people who run marathons know it, at least if they do it on a daily basis.

At the end of the day, the last thing you want to do is make yourself a cup of coffee, let alone clean a rifle or do sentry duty out in front of the machine gun.

The others in the patrol feel the same, they must. I look at "Smithy" my mate who I've been sharing a "hole in the ground" with, for the last two months. Fortunately he's making the coffee, I just don't have the energy but that is the way it works during operations. Some days it would be me who had the energy.

This operation started three weeks ago and there are another two weeks to go. There will only be four or five hours sleep a night followed by the next day, looking for Charlie. Then the pleasure of two shifts of two hours on night sentry duty.

You just want to lay down and sleep. But you can't. So you light up a cigarette and get ready for your turn as sentry.

I'm leaning against my pack, with my eyes closed willing myself to stand up, when Smithy says, "There's your brew" as he hands me a mug of coffee then continues, "I'll swap your shift, you can have a gonk (sleep)" he says as he walks towards the sentry position outside the perimeter. What a relief. I get a break.
I noticed his empty mug with dregs of black coffee.
We both only ever drank our coffee with condensed milk. The sugar was essential for the energy and I could see the empty tube of condensed milk rolled up in a ball.
Smithy had given me the last of our condensed milk, which was no big deal.
After all, Smithy was a mate.

189

JULY 1969
UNAUTHORISED DISCHARGES

By the time we had two months in-country, we developed a cadence of life which went something like, planning and preparation, carry out the operation followed by a couple of days rest. The "rest" normally included the consumption of mind-boggling quantities of alcohol and occasional exotic cigarettes after which we started the cycle all over again.

As a part of preparation we would test fire our weapons on the rifle range. Often this was nothing more than what came to be called a "yippee shoot", where we could blast away with hundreds of rounds of automatic fire.

This part of the preparation phase for most of us, often came within hours the last glass or joint or both, therefore concentration and gross motor coordination was often minimal. These test firing sessions were often accidents waiting to happen, with around thirty soldiers mostly hung over, each carrying a couple of hundred rounds of ammunition it was only a matter of time there was an accidental firing or what the army euphemistically called an Unauthorised Discharge.

In fact, originally these were called accidental discharges until some soldiers started losing the plot, firing at anyone or anything with nothing accidental in their method. Just a way to let of steam. Since this was not cool and there was nothing accidental about the way some soldiers were firing their weapons, the army decided to cover all contingencies and changed the wording to Unauthorised Discharges.

Presumably, if some-one senior lost it and started ordering soldiers to shoot our own, this would be regarded as authorised and cool. On more than one occasion during one of these "test firings" we had near misses. One memorable incident occurred while we were preparing for our second operation. As the platoon commander was loading a couple of magazines, I was watching him and fiddling with the safety catch on my rifle.

For some unknown reason, thinking my weapon was unloaded, I squeezed the trigger. Needless to say there was a loud bang as the round kicked up the dirt, centimetres from the skipper's foot. This was followed by stunned silence from everyone while a pale faced platoon commander said "Right, "Titch", you're on a charge for an unauthorised discharge".

Some two weeks later, Ray, a corporal from another section who shared the same tent as me was preparing for a patrol. Ray picked up a rifle believing it to be his and pointed it at me, saying, "Don't worry, I always know whether or not my weapon is loaded; not like you"! He was laughing as he squeezed the trigger, moving the rifle to one side so as not to point it directly at me. There was a loud explosion in the confined space of the tent as the bullet missed me by millimetres, making a hole in the tent. The rifle belonged to someone else.

AUGUST 1969
THE MEASUREMENT OF TIME

There was the obsession with time, that is, how much time one had left before the twelve month "Tour of Duty" was finished. It should be remembered that anyone serving in the field was in survival mode; i.e. to finish the tour was to win. So much so that some had the numbers from 365 to 0 written on their hats crossing off the numbers as each day passed. Understandably, this obsession was manifested everywhere, on the walls of tents, buildings.

Even in some of the phraseology, so that when someone was described as short it was not a description of height, rather it referred to the length of time left to serve in-country. If someone was long they were recently arrived and perhaps not as reliable as a "Short Timer" who had much more experience. Paradoxically, if a soldier was very short then he may have been totally unreliable.

191

After all, getting killed or wounded in the last few weeks of a tour, seemed so dumb.

This led to what soldiers today, in Iraq and Afghanistan, refer to as the "Koala Bear Syndrome". That is, just sit there in the tree and don't move. If you do nothing, you have less chance of being killed. Quite simple really.

Finally, there was even a chart with 365 dots, in the form of a large breasted woman. Each dot had a number in the figure of a woman with the last day or ZERO, unknowingly, but strategically placed on what would be familiar to most high school students today, as the G spot.

SEPTEMBER 1969
HONOUR AND DISHONOUR

Tattoos on the forearm with "Death Before Dishonour" were quite common although seen less often towards the end of the tour. Not because the wearer of the tattoo got his wish. More likely because as the days passed, war became the reality of killing and dying. Never mind the obvious lack of any honour in jungle warfare with napalm, land mines and Agent Orange courtesy of the West and Punji pits, Booby traps and more land mines, courtesy of the East.

Under those circumstances it was more honourable to keep the sleeves rolled down and come back home alive. Near the end, honour was in very short supply.

PHILOSOPHY IN A TENT

It was poring down when Johno came into our tent at the base in Nui Dat.
"Hey Titch, what are you writing?" Asked Johno.
"Just some stuff for my diary", I replied
"Well", said Johno, "This whole war is crap, you know this Communist stuff is like, well these Nogs have got nothing and

they want to share it with everybody. Like a bloody race where everybody comes first without a prize. I mean we've been here five fucking months and what have we done? Sweet fuck all mate, sweet fuck all. There you are Titch; put that in your diary"

OCTOBER 1969
A PRISONER AND A CROCODILE

Radio transmission after a contact:
"This is Sunray, sitrep over"
"Send your sitrep over",
"We have no friendly casualties, one enemy POW and one enemy EBC over".
"Roger. What do mean EBC? Over".
"Eaten by crocodile! (Referring to a half eaten corpse in the river)" Over.

NOVEMBER 1969
NICK NAMES

After about six months in country, everyone had a nick name and the real name was hardly ever used. Tall people were called "Lofty", occasionally though they were called "Shorty". Nearly everyone with red hair was called "Blue".

Although more often than not, the nick name was some version of the family name, a shortened version of their first name or through some connection with their function within the unit. It was all up to the imagination.

The Trackers had a range of nick names which would have been typical of any Infantry unit.

The platoon commander was called "Skipper", although if he had to make a tough decision which we didn't like, even if it was the right one, we referred to him as "Never Root", which was derived from his family name "Neervoort".

193

The platoon Sergeant who's family name was Buttegieg, was called "Butch". I don't know why, but I noticed that if we were very drunk his family name would sound something like "Buteecheig", so Butch was easier, drunk or sober.

There was a bloke with the family name Kohn who was called "Kahoona", another one with the name of Puie, was called "Pubes" or his full nick name, "Pubic Hair".

There was another with the nickname of "Thongs" which referred to his love of thongs. You see if one had a medical certificate to wear thongs you couldn't wear boots and therefore could not go out on operations. A very sane approach to a tricky situation.

Someone who didn't eat much would be called "Fang". We had another bloke called "Lefty" whose real name was Neville, which had absolutely no connection with the real name. Although if I remember correctly, he had a pretty good left hook.

In fact over time there was nobody who was called by their real name. There was a kind anonymity. The only people who used the real name were ones who did not belong to your platoon. It was your mates or those who you worked with knew your nick name.

There were of course those with generic nick names which signified their work. For instance, soldiers posted to the Hygiene Section, which had the important job of mosquito control and latrine maintenance were called "Turd Burglars" or "Blowflies". Needless to say that regardless of how important it was few soldiers volunteered for this posting.

The Military Police were called "Meat Heads" after the red berets they wore, while the Artillery were called "Drop Shorts", implying a lack of accuracy which resulted in so called "Friendly Fire". In fact, most instances were due to poor map reading on the part of the person calling in the fire.

Armoured Corps were referred to as "Turret Heads", "Tankies or "Rectum Rangers", which was the result of a "small scandal" which occurred during a training exercise. Not much imagination needed for this name.

Effectively, nicknames were not only a way of shortening communication time, but an indication that you were part of the group.

DECEMBER 1969
A MEMORABLE CHRISTMAS

The sound of Christmas carols greeted me, as I woke up through the blurry vista of fever in sweat soaked sheets.

Two days earlier, a Medevac helicopter had deposited me at the field hospital after being hoisted through the trees during a hair raising extraction from the May Tao mountains. By the time I arrived at the field hospital in Vung Tau, on the 20th of December, I had a serious case of hepatitis and was barely able to function.

Hepatitis put me as the only occupant of the isolation ward, which was more a like a form of solitary confinement, except for the fact that everyone who came into the room, was completely covered and wore masks and gloves.

The sound of Christmas carols continued as I listened and watched through the window as all the medical staff and patients, gathered around the beds of those who were too ill to move. There was an obvious irony in the middle of all this madness. The carols with their underlying message of peace, sung by the servants of war. Then they started singing "Silent Night", probably the only carol of which I knew the words. I cried.

JANUARY 1970
A VALUED PROMOTION

When I had Hepatitis, while the CO was visiting the sick and wounded in hospital, we had a short conversation in which he said to me, "When you get out of hospital you won't be going back to the Trackers. You'll be sent to 3 Platoon as a section commander".

"Thanks very much sir". I replied. After all, it was what I wanted.

FEBRUARY 1970
AN UNFORTUNATE UNDERESTIMATION

FEBRUARY 26:
Patrol briefing for 3 platoon A Company, Radio call sign "one three", at approx. 1700hrs.

Section Commander; "So what's the deal with the Nogs?"
Platoon Commander; "Intelligence reckons there could be the heavy weapons company of D445 Battalion. Obviously if they thought the information was serious they wouldn't be sending an under strength platoon like ours to check out a Company of enemy"
Section Commander; "Right, well there's only two more days then we are back for a rest, bloody boring chasing around with bullshit intelligence".

FEBRUARY 28:

Forward scout: "This is crap, there's no bastard out here".
Section Commander: "Yea, well let's go on for another half hour then I'll ask the boss for a break.
Exchange between section commander and scout at approx. 1600hrs.

"One this is one three - contact! Wait out".
Radio Operator call sign one three, reporting contact with VC/NVA at approx. 1630hrs.

Radio Transmissions at approx. 1730hrs between A Company Headquarters and 3 Platoon one hour after initial contact.

"One three this is One, fetch Sunray over". (HQ Asking for the Platoon Commander).
"This is One Three, Sunray is WIA over". (Commander Wounded In Action) and we have figures one zero, 10 WIA".
"One three this is one say again your WIA over" (wounded in action)
"This is one three, I say again, we have figures one zero 10, WIA", over.
"This is one, are you saying you have figures one zero, 10 WIA", over.
"This is one three, that's affirmative, it may be more" over.
"This is one, wait out", A company headquarters digesting information.

MARCH 1970
REALITY

The Age newspaper, Melbourne March 2nd. 1970, report datelined "Saigon February 28th. 1970"
38 Australian Casualties
"9 diggers killed and 15 wounded by mines.
Another 14 wounded by rocket propelled grenades and machine gun fire".

A BIRTHDAY
March 5

Six days previously, I had been deposited once again, at the field hospital along with the rest of my section. Once again after another hair raising, this time at night, hot extraction.

Like many in my section, I had been in and out of the operating theatre as the medical teams worked to save our arses. In my case literally.

After all that, I had been full of morphine for nearly a week and the only reason I knew it was my birthday, was because the

197

staff and some of the patients were singing happy birthday and there was a cake in front of me.

One of the medics slipped me a massive rum and coke, which combined with the morphine put me in orbit around another planet. I am sure it was the best birthday party I have forgotten. I still can't remember much of it.

LEAVING
March 10

They all came down to say goodbye, the CO, the Trackers and 3 Platoon. It was pretty nice. The best moment was when one of the Trackers said, "Come on Titch, give us a look at your arse".
So I rolled over and displayed my "Ticket Home". A long incision from the front of my hip bone to the base of my spine where a "Dum Dum" had literally shredded the upper portion of my left buttock.
"Bloody hell!" exclaimed the skipper, "Just missed your brains".
We all laughed, even though it hurt, I couldn't stop, it was really funny.
I was going home.

22

FLASHBACK

"There was a feeling of deja vu; I had already tried to forget this".

It is near the end of the monsoon season, with the black clouds rolling across the bay, along the Back Beach at Vung Tau. The massive thunder heads have started to let loose their daily deluge, a spectacle of nature that is the monsoon. Every now and then, there are massive sheets of lightning followed by loud thunder claps. It has been like this since I arrived here ten days ago, just as it was forty years ago, the first time I was here.

Of course then, the sounds of thunder and rain were augmented with the sounds of artillery, mortars and helicopters. Today these have been replaced with the sounds of motorbikes and cars as people go about their business. There is still the occasional helicopter, but these days they are Russian helicopters, which ferry workers to and from the oil rigs located miles off the Southern Vietnamese coast.

The decision to visit and write this chapter of this book in Vietnam was a deliberate one. Not based on guilt or deep nostalgia, but probably more on a sense of curiosity. To see how the place had changed and to make some sense of the events that happened all those years ago. Perhaps, like many who have been in war, there is also the search for reconciliation when one walks over the ground of old battlefields.

To come here at the end of the monsoon was also a deliberate decision. For most of us the wet season was the hardest of our war in Vietnam. Apart from the discomfort of always being wet, it gave Charlie some respite, since the weather conditions restricted the use of our helicopters and artillery. This neutralised our advantage as well as creating the most difficult conditions to live in, let alone to try and fight a war.

The monsoon is Asia at its most evocative. Strong enough to clarify many of those forgotten memories, which have been edited and sifted away. Not only that, but the monsoon seems to intensify the feeling of how much change has taken place during the intervening years.

Vung Tau as it was when we first came here, ceased to exist more than ten years ago. While I expected to find little to jog the memory here, it would be a good base from which I could go and visit some of the places where we looked for and sometimes encountered Charlie. Although, in retrospect, it was more likely that he found us and we just didn't know it.

Fortunately, for my time here, I found a small house for rent, on the hill overlooking the Back Beach at Vung Tau. Tran the owner, was typical of the new generation of Vietnamese, the ideology of Communism was long gone. Over a couple of beers on my first evening, Tran explained the modern day Vietnamese point of view to me; "Simply put, we are a Communist country with eighty-six million capitalists", he said with a laugh and continued, "My father was in the war and in the end, nobody was very interested who won, they just wanted the war to finish and the foreigners to leave".

"But do the Vietnamese have any deep opinion about the war?" I asked.
Tran smiled and said, "Well we won, so for us it is not so important, except for some Vietnamese who work in tourism. They show the foreigners some places where there was fighting and keep alive some old ideology, but that is only because they make money from this".

We shared our thoughts on this for a while as the shadows lengthened until suddenly, it was pitch black with only the sound of the geckos, insects and the rain drumming lightly on the roof.

"I should go to my family" said Tran

"Yes of course" I said, "If you want we can catch up in a couple of days".

"Ok, that would be nice", he replied as he walked away into the darkness.

That night going to sleep was easy, with the noises of the night interspersed with the distant sound of the waves on the beach. There was a sense of anticipation as I looked forward to exploring the new Vung Tau and perhaps finding some of the old places, within the present day atmosphere of the resort city that Vung Tau is today. During those initial days, it seemed that there was no evidence of the past. However, if I looked carefully amongst the modern trappings of tourism, there were small reminders of the past.

There was the occasional bicycle, overloaded with bags of fruit or rice on the verge of falling over, pushed along by a struggling slightly built Vietnamese. No different to the way the previous generation moved supplies from one village to another or down the Ho Chi Minh trail.

There were occasional small groups of older men on low stools drinking sickly sweet coffee and smoking huge rolls of tobacco leaf, as they did in years gone by. Other than that there was little to remind one of the past.

A couple of days later, as I was walking along Tran Phu Boulevard, I lost count of the four and five star hotels. Further along towards the back beach there were more than a dozen multi storey hotels with air-conditioned coffee shops and souvenir shops to cater for the burgeoning tourist market.

In the centre of all this activity, I noticed a bar called the "Kangaroo Bar", followed by "The Etta Restaurant" and "The

Good Old Aussie Pie Shop", a demonstration of the relatively strong presence of ex patriot Australians who had set up businesses here. A little further on, there was "Bellys Bar" from which echoed the sounds of laughter followed by Australian accents, which I had to follow inside.

There were about twenty people, nearly all of a certain age and it didn't take long to understand that most of them were veterans of the Vietnam War. That this was their place was highlighted by the photos and mementos hung on the wall. These had been donated by other veterans, who had travelled through here over the last few years. Along the wall the photos were the usual ones, of young soldiers still naïve enough to believe in their own invincibility. Then, in the far corner I noticed a montage of photos in a large frame. Amongst the photos were the two tracker dogs, Julian and Janus, which had been used by Five Battalion. Yet another small memorial to the tracker dogs.

While most of the people at "Bellys" were veterans, they were in fact, a very small minority of the nearly 45,000 Australian soldiers who served in Vietnam. They had decided to live in the "Fantasy of Nam". They had chosen to live "in country" only a "couple of clicks" out of town on their "second tour", a tour of duty for life. It seemed a conscious decision to live in the past and view life, through the hazy prism of alcohol, with a "clearing patrol" every morning to pick up the empties of the night before. Not the way to live for most of us, but I suppose it is understandable.

If one had preconceptions and wanted to see the "Nam" of a stereotypical "Authentic Vet" like the one born out of films, through the eyes of an inarticulate Rambo, then this could be the most likely place. Although it would only be emblematic, of a year lost in Vietnam and not much else. Perhaps it was not so much living in a fantasy but rather a way of touching that atmosphere of war, which for some can be quite addictive. More likely though, it was the desperate yearning that most men have, for the energy and invincibility of a youth long gone.

The "69 Bar cum Steam Bath and Hairdresser" still exists, however these days it has transformed into a small franchising operation, in a very different form or perhaps "Re-branded" would be a better word. Today it is just "The 69 Bar" and there are now three of them, one in Hanoi and Saigon, with the third in Vung Tau. "Haircuts and Exotic Massages" are no longer advertised or available, although good food and wine is. The one in Hanoi is recommended by guide books as a sophisticated restaurant and bar. The "Belle of Baria" and the other girls who "worked" here, would be out of place these days. Although I have no doubt that with her style and capacity to survive, the Belle of Baria would have easily adapted to the change in ambiance.

The Grand hotel is still there, now as a genuine five star hotel, occupying a large chunk of prime real estate near the beach. Similar services are offered, as they were in the past. The girls dressed in their traditional ao dais offer an alluring glimpse of what might be available. These days that is all, just a glimpse. Obviously the Bong, Blow job, Beer and Blue movie that made up the Four B's for four dollars, are no longer on offer and the massages no longer come with a happy ending.

Riding a motorbike through the traffic around Vung Tau is just as chaotic as it was decades ago. The Vespa motor scooters have been replaced by swarms of Honda motorbikes, slipping in and out of impossibly narrow gaps like bees swarming between the large drones that are the ungainly four wheel drives. The traffic lights are still only a form of advice, with a choice to stop when the lights are red, or sail on blithely through the oncoming traffic. Of course the same applies if the lights are green, it's just advice. At first glance the traffic flow seems totally without rhyme or reason. Eventually, however, there is the realization that it flows seamlessly, like water, finding its way around impassable rocks.

The rules are never broken rather they are bent, like bamboo, which if something goes wrong, will come back with a swift and stinging blow. Usually in the form of immediate financial compensation for the injured party, or an "On the Spot Bribe" to an ever smiling policeman. It is similar to our system which has no bribe but which is more than made up for, with the much larger fine, to cover the expensive bureaucracy in the middle. In the end you still have to pay.

It seems to me that the essence of the people in Vietnam has some expression in the traffic. In this case that essence is tolerance. Tolerance for the bike on the wrong side of the road or for the large truck ignoring the traffic lights and applying "the law of the biggest" which allows, up to a certain point, the biggest to do whatever they want. This form of tolerance, which we had misread as weakness, is probably one of the greatest strengths that exist in Asia. That is the strength of patience, the willingness to bend with the strength of bamboo, which will tolerate a state of war for years to achieve victory.

About half a kilometre along the Back Beach boulevard, was our old leave centre The Badcoe Club, which has been replaced by the multi-story four star "Imperial Hotel". The only reason I could be certain of this, is because I could see a large section of the old tarmac a few metres away on which there was the faded white outline of the landing circle for the helicopter LZ used for the field hospital. As I walked slowly along the length of the LZ, as if on cue, an old Russian ML8 Helicopter flew overhead towards the sea with its load of oil workers. I guess the noise of the chopper did it. Whatever it was, I stood there on the tarmac, thinking about that night when five of us arrived at the doorstep of the field hospital in a helicopter. The inside of which, would have looked like an abattoir killing floor, since we had all spent the previous half hour flopping around, bleeding like stuck pigs. It was a bloody day in February 1970. The Australians had nine killed in action and twenty seven wounded that day. It was a moment when I understood that sometimes it is possible to feel past events.

My thoughts were interrupted by a young Vietnamese boy of about fourteen on a bicycle, who smiled at me and asked, "Where you come from?"

"From Uc, Uc Daloi; Australia, I am Australian", I replied with the few words of Vietnamese I could remember.

"Ha! Uc Daloi, cheap charlie", he said with a laugh as he cycled off, repeating again the phrase which greeted nearly all Australian soldiers in Vietnam who had a reputation as hard bargainers with very deep pockets. It would seem that the ex patriot Australians have maintained the same standard for a new generation of Vietnamese.

My first few days had been more than useful, since I had the opportunity of acclimatising to the local traffic on a rented Honda "Dream" motorbike, before visiting some of the places up towards our old base at Nui Dat.

Later in the evening Tran came over with a new map of the province along with some tips on the quicker routes to and from the surrounding villages. Before he left he said, "I spoke to my father about you and he would like to meet you, if you have the time".

"Sure", I replied, "Maybe tomorrow evening.

"Ok, I pick you up and we have dinner at my family's home".

That was perfect. Like many soldiers from old wars, in the aftermath, there is always the residual curiosity of the enemy's point of view.

Early next morning I made my way on the Honda motorbike to the village of Long Hai, a few kilometres further down the coast. This would be my first stop. After which I would complete a loop, through Baria and back down to Vung Tau. The "village" of Long Hai is no longer a collection of a few huts, rather a more substantial group of houses with an expensive seaside resort and spa nearby, where one can be pampered for an eye watering price of $350.00 per day. Long Hai itself was not so important. It was more of a reference point from where I would head north along the road which ran parallel to the Long Hai mountains on my left. Given the memories associated with the Long Hai Mountains and the "Light Green", the presence of a luxury resort a couple of kilometres away, seemed all the more incongruous. The two names that, for the Australians, were synonymous with land mines and the internal fear that came with a patrol in the open fields of "The Light Green". These days "The Light Green" is devoted to rice farming with a few buffalo grazing contentedly. It is hard to believe that the last time I was here, there were land mines scattered all over the place. The mines which gave rise to more than a thousand Australian casualties. I was about a kilometre away from the mountains which put me roughly where "Fire Support Base Thrust" would have been.

At this point I stopped and left the bike to take a walk around. There was a sense of the surreal to be walking the same ground that we were on decades before, made more poignant with the names of those I knew, who had their lives changed or cut short in these fields. The names came back readily enough. Darby, Bushy, Doc, Needsie and there must have been twenty more names that I didn't know, who became casualties in that bloody month of July 1969. There was, of course, Tinh, the Bushman Scout, one of the bravest, who one year after we left, stood on a mine and had his legs blown away.

After an hour or so, I left, riding towards Baria. It took at least half an hour to clear away the depressive thoughts that came with the Long Hais. There was no way to find something positive in this. When it comes to land mines and war, there is just a sense of pointless waste. As I entered Baria, I realised that the village no longer existed. It was more like a city with a new four lane highway. It was unrecognisable and it took me a while to find the

North South road on which I would travel tomorrow to have a look at our old base Nui Dat and some of the places of our first serious operation.

The sky was full of huge black clouds as I rode back to Vung Tau, hoping to make it before the daily deluge, I was on the last two kilometres when rain came down in sheets with the thunder and lighting providing the daily spectacle of nature.

Sometime later, as we arranged, Tran came and took me to the family house a couple of hundred metres further up the hill. When we neared the house he turned and said, "You know it's not often that my father has any contact with our guests".

"I guess we have at least one thing in common", I replied with a small laugh.

Tran smiled and said, "My father has met a few foreigners who fought in the war, but this is the first time we have had one of you staying here". Tran continued, "Tonight there will be my wife and our two children as well as my brother and his wife, so you will see a typical Vietnamese family dinner, we always seem to have the extended part of the family", he trailed off the sentence as he motioned me through the front door to a sort of ante room where as is the custom we took off our shoes.

We then moved into a large room which served as a kitchen, dining room and lounge room. In one corner the TV was on though no one was really watching. It provided a sort of background noise as the family was scattered around the room where the children played while the adults were engaged in lively conversation around a large dining table. The room became quiet as Tran introduced me, first to his father then the other adults and children. When he had finished, his brother Nguyen said, "Tran and I will have to translate for you because the others don't speak much English".

"That's no problem, I'm sure it's better than my Vietnamese", I said ironically as the brothers laughed.

There was the initial awkwardness that is always present, with a different language and culture. However, after about half an hour the conversation flowed smoothly enough with the two brothers translating. All of this was made easier by the fact that they had cousins who were living in Australia. As Tran's father spoke, everyone stopped talking.

Tran translated, "He wants to know when you were here".

"In 1969 and '70, we operated out of the base at Nui Dat".

"And what did you do?" asked Tran.

At this point we were sizing each other up, like two dogs, warily sniffing each other.

It was in the typical way of soldiers, trying to understand and see if there was common ground. The difference between infantry soldiers who have been exposed to combat and soldiers who have not, would offer less common ground and there is a very different "Smell" between a "Pogo" and an infantry "Grunt". It didn't take long to establish that we had shared similar experiences, although on opposite sides.

Tran's father continued, "This is the first time I have shared a meal with someone from the other side of the war".

"Actually, it's the same for me", I replied. "And what exactly did you do?" I asked.

He then explained that he was part of the system whereby the local Viet Cong would use people like him, with local knowledge as guides, for North Vietnamese units moving through the province. Work with a fair amount of danger given the continuous exposure to Australian "enemy" patrols searching for "Charlie".

As the evening moved on, between the food, beer and rice wine, we swapped stories, while Tran and his brother translated. Everybody was silent as Tran's father described some of his operations with the children wide-eyed, at what they perceived as a scary adventure story. Through the evening there was the sense that while we were not the same, we were similar, at least we had shared similar dangers and discomforts, generic to any form of infantry work.

It was late in the evening and although we could have continued for hours longer, our translators were tiring. By the time I stood up to leave it was well after midnight.

We shook hands once more and before leaving Tran's father invited me to return whenever I wanted to. Tran translated, "My father says that he is always here in the late afternoon, so you can come up whenever you feel like". I accepted with the issue of translation seeming less relevant. There was a sense of the surreal in all of this. Not so long ago, the idea that decades after the war, I would be dining with and sharing stories in the convivial atmosphere of the home and family of a Viet Cong, would have been inconceivable. It was a nice evening.

The following day I left after a late breakfast, along the road that ran roughly North/South towards Baria and Nui Dat. There was a two lane highway all the way up from Vung Tau, which sliced like a black ribbon through the rice paddies and small villages that are typical of anywhere in Vietnam.

Riding through the occasional cluster of houses, the clash of rural past and industrial present was underlined by a young kid on a water buffalo waving to me, as the latest BMW flashed past. A little further on a shopkeeper was talking on a mobile phone, while half a dozen people dressed in black pyjamas and wearing the ubiquitous pointy hats they call nonlas, were working in the field bobbing up and down like giant mushrooms.

Coming up along the main North South road, I recognised the rising ground and the outline of "SAS Hill" behind the main gate which was the entrance to the base. I turned off following the road to the right of the hill, until I arrived at a strip of tarmac which was "Kangaroo Pad". It was from here that we had boarded the choppers for our various operations and unless you knew the history, it looked rather insignificant. About five hundred metres further on and around to the left, I was directly in line with SAS Hill which was roughly where we had our base. It was difficult to know the exact location, because the whole area is now a functioning rubber plantation. However a few minutes later I found the marker stone and flag pole stand, which indicated the location of Battalion Headquarters. With that I was able to find exactly where the Trackers and the kennels were all those years ago. I walked on past what would have been the location of the "Chew it and Spew it" mess or dining hall, where we had some of the wildest alcohol fuelled nights, followed the next day by some rather ordinary food for breakfast. Although the quality of the food was partially rectified one morning by "Crazy Kev" when he decided to take to the cook responsible with the creative use of a soup ladle.

Further on there still remained some cement flooring which was part of the 6RAR kennels, the home of Trajan, Marcus and Milo, who between them prevented many Australian casualties all long gone, to be with the emperors after whom they were named. The memory of Trajan, standing with his head cocked to one side waiting for the gate to be opened, is crystal clear. Not far, perhaps two hundred metres further on, slightly to the left of the kennels, was the place where we had set up our tents as the Trackers. The rubber trees cast long straight shadows as I walked between them, up to a large open patch of ground, which was just behind where our "Skull Cave" would have been, where we had the occasional drunken sing-along with "Charlie".

It would have been somewhere around here, that they buried "Charlie". The sun had dried out yesterday's monsoon rain and shone brightly, as a breeze picked up, creating a small whirlwind of dust which moved around the open patch of ground. The small whirlwind went around for what seemed like at least a minute, as it danced over the open ground coming right up to me, then stopping beside my foot. The breeze then died down leaving an atmosphere of quiet peace. What was that about? "Charlie"?

Maybe it was him, just saying hello. That's the thing about Charlie, you could never be sure, this was after all his place.

Coming around to the right of the hill, I left Nui Dat riding along the old airstrip that was Luscombe Field, which was the landing strip used by fixed wing aircraft. The tarmac is now part of a road, lined by houses on each side, which runs through the rubber plantation at Nui Dat today. There is little left of our presence here years ago and the place is probably better for that.

When I arrived once more at the main North South Road, I turned right towards the village of Binh Ba and the Courtney rubber plantation. This was where we had conducted our first so called warm up "Nursery Operation" and where, in June of '69, 5 Battalion had a fairly large battle at Binh Ba with the 33rd North Vietnamese Regiment. At that time, we were about ten kilometres further north of Binh Ba, at fire support base Virginia in an area known as the "Courtney Rubber". As the North Vietnamese moved away from the battle at Binh Ba, many of them bumped into us. As a consequence our "Nursery Operation" turned into a series of full-on contacts, with dogs being deployed on follow up tracks and having our first contact with Charlie.

It would be an exaggeration to say that after all these years I was able to find our original fire support base, but after riding down several side roads, I eventually found the approximate location of our area of operations. I had been walking around through the rubber trees for about half an hour when I realised that there was nothing left to recognise and nothing left to remember.

It was time to go home.

By the time I returned to the small house in Vung Tau, the daily deluge had just started and the rain was hammering away on the roof of the veranda. The monsoon rain always provided enjoyable moments of reflection, given one was under cover and not subjected to attacks by leeches or mosquitoes.

How natural it seemed then, to be here in the midst of war and how improbable it all seems now. As young soldiers we had little sense of proportion or probability and no experience on which to base our decisions or judgements. Our only certainty was that we were invincible, as all young men are and if someone was going to be a casualty, it would always be someone else.

William Prochnau's book, "Once Upon a Distant War", described Vietnam as "Exotic, Erotic and Narcotic", and in retrospect it probably was an apt description. Perhaps because these days, after more years passing, our war becomes more distant. We talk about Vietnam with an increasingly wistful nostalgia, as if there is a search for new "heroes" still living, to replace the ones now dead.

There is no doubt that for some of us, once the smell of war reached the nostrils, we would spend the rest of our lives searching for that same scent. Not to find a war, that was the last thing we wanted to do. Rather to find that feeling of high adventure that comes with the rush of adrenaline associated with an objective element of danger. The type of danger which creates the area known in Tibetan Buddhism as "The Bardo", the space between life and death. It is this space which allows some of us to know that we are alive. The same atmosphere that is often found in extreme sports, such as mountaineering, or with travel in the remote regions of the world or in occupations which have a high level of physical and mental stress. Through which it is possible to have a sense of identity and belonging to a team.

Interlinked with this, is the sense of trust between people who choose to place themselves in situations of objective danger. A sense of trust that can never be found in the everyday world, where money has to be earned and the rule of "Caveat Emptor" is the basis for survival. These are all things that are experiential and for most people, difficult to understand or explain, and better understood retrospectively.

Amongst all of these reflections, the last few hours in Vung Tau were spent packing my gear, ready for an early morning departure to Ton Son Nhut airport, for my flight back home. There was also a long and pleasant interruption when I went up to see Tran and say goodbye to his family who had looked after me so well and more particularly to present Tran's father with a small gift, a Zhi bead, one of the symbols of Buddhism, which I knew he would recognise.

When I arrived, the deluge had become a drizzle and Tran's father was sitting on the veranda watching the ship traffic on the bay, through the mist of rain. He nodded and smiled as he went inside and returned with a pot of green tea. Over the last week, this had become an almost daily ritual between Tran's father and me. The tea would be poured and we would sit together for quite a while, with the silence interrupted by the occasional sound of thunder. That was all. There never seemed to be the need to say anything.

So maybe there was no deep opinion from the other side. Just the camaraderie of two soldiers who had lived through the same war.

When the tea was finished I went inside and said my goodbyes to the rest of the family and accepted Tran's offer to drive me to the airport early the next morning. I gave Tran's father the Zhi bead which he recognised immediately for the Buddha talisman that it was. He smiled and at the same moment handed me an old, small Buddha statue. Both are similar to a talisman, not to bring good luck, rather to help avoid bad luck. For many people, the talisman has always been important, especially for soldiers who are not superstitious.

As I walked back I couldn't help thinking that at a macro and political level there is that great gulf of misunderstanding that exists between Asia and us. But at a micro level, person to person, the gulf is a small gap which in the end can be bridged without a spoken word. As two old soldiers, once enemies, are able to sit together in silence. We shared similar experiences and difficulties from which we developed a mutual respect that comes with that understanding. The silence was enough.

It seemed that I had only a couple of hours sleep, when Tran was knocking on my door with his car ready to take me to the airport. We left Vung Tau as the sun rose and a little more than an hour later Tran was helping me with my gear to the check in counter. As we walked towards Immigration there was the usual awkward moment as we said goodbye.

Tran looked at me directly and said, "You know you have a place any time you want".

There was not much else to say except, "Thanks".

As I walked through the sliding doors, I turned to wave and Tran said, "Hey Uc Daloi, I see you later"

"You will", I replied, "You will".

Clearing immigration and customs was quiet and efficient in the newly renovated Ton Son Nhut Airport and it wasn't long before we were on board and ready for takeoff. The new and nearly full Airbus climbed out of Saigon and turned South East towards Australia.

How things change.

I was surrounded by Vietnamese, mainly young, most of who spoke Australian accented English. Many would have to be children of those who fled Vietnam in flimsy boats as refugees when the war was lost.

As I thought about the changes in Vietnam, which are evident today, I realised that they probably started around the time that the film, "Indochine" was released. This film was not the only catalyst but it certainly added to the already growing interest in a Vietnam that had just opened its doors to foreign tourists. Not only from the young adventurous backpackers from Europe but also the United States, where the film added to the growing curiosity from a younger generation, about the American participation in a far away war.

The film was a wide ranging exotic arc of French colonial history, in some way a French answer to Kipling's India.

Whatever the reason, "Indochine" certainly galvanised the tourist industry, in similar way that "Passage to India" created a post colonial nostalgia in the sub-continent, for a non-existent past.

Never the less, they came in droves, searching for the "Authentic, Exotic and Erotic, Nam Experience".

They were assisted by travel agents, who could never see the irony, of promoting the most heavily bombed country in history; as unspoiled. "The discerning traveller should go there before it was ruined" was the marketing publicity and so they came in their thousands, to view a Vietnam, which was no longer a war but a country. Of course the initial curiosity was about "Nam", the war, not so much about Vietnam the country.

Although Australians rarely used the word "Nam", it was eventually adopted from the Americans. Regardless of the Rambo like connotation, there is no doubt that the very word "Nam", evokes images of smoke filled opium dens, music from The Doors, "Napalm in the morning" and a slinky bar girl sound track in the background of , "No money no honey, give me ten dollars I love you long time'.

From the mid nineties until today, the majority of tourists have come for that "Authentic Nam Experience", which has been provided for by the development of sites, like the "Cu Chi" tunnels, a sort of paradoxical "Cong World", the only thing missing is a giant VC statue; similar to the type of self promotion that one sees in Queensland, like the giant pineapple.

The tunnels are more like a series of ironic contradictions, after all their importance during the war was their invisibility and inaccessibility. Most of the occupants were guerrillas who were highly mobile and unencumbered. Obviously these qualities are a hindrance to a tourist attraction, so the tunnels have been made semi-visible, while a big show is made of their invisibility. Such as when a guide uncovers a hidden entrance, cunningly disguised with leaves glued together with raw latex from nearby rubber trees.

215

For a more profound experience, one can crawl through some 40 metres of tunnel, which was originally very narrow to keep large westerners out and has since been widened, to allow mostly overweight westerner the doubtful privilege of a claustrophobic experience.

There is also a rather decrepit rifle range, where for ten dollars one can fire a few rounds with a Kalashnikov rifle. The rifle is attached to a bench by a heavy metal chain about twenty centimetres long, doubtless to prevent any deranged veteran wanting to swing around with a ten round burst to avenge a long lost war.

This experience can be followed up by a tour where one can see, the not so well hidden tunnel entrances and trip wires which set off fire crackers. The tour is finished off with a "VC Meal" of manioc with peanuts and green tea as one listens to the tour guide describe life from the other side during the war in "Nam" while he shows some grainy black and white photos of "American war crimes".

In the attempt to become more authentic, Cong World has had to add new layers of falsehood to feed the ever credulous tourist.
In the end Cong World and The War Crimes Museum are just fading memories and losing their relevance. It is more than twenty years since Cong World and other ancillary tourist attractions such as the War Crimes Museum were opened to attract tourists.

Since then, there has been a distinct toning down of the rhetoric. Cong World has few visitors these days and the American War Crimes Museum has been renamed, more realistically, The War Remnants museum, with a water puppet show in the evenings.
"Nam" no longer has any real place for the Vietnamese.

Certainly a search of the libraries and the internet will reveal thousands of volumes about "Nam". From a complete list of war dead, to a list of bars, with names like "B52" and "B4-75" with cocktails of the same name, still trying to maintain the atmosphere of "Cong World".

Effectively these days, the "Nam" of Vietnam is for the aficionados of an old war, who want to see Vietnam through the prism of "Nam" and these are few in number.

Today the others who know the real Vietnam are the young, who leave the stories of "Nam" to much older men, grandfathers or great uncles who every now and then have a young audience that will sit, enthralled, at the repeated stories of a great adventure, which has always been the view of war by the young.

Because no matter how much the stories are down played or how often they are told, they will always seem larger than life even if they are, by now, very old.

As the plane reached cruising altitude the young Vietnamese flight attendant asked me, in perfect English, if I would like some tea or coffee. I couldn't help feeling that there was some irony in all of this. After all, the last time I flew out of Vietnam it was on an Australian Air force Medical Evacuation flight, with a broken hip and a shredded arse, courtesy of a couple of well aimed shots from "Charlie".

Yes, no doubt about it, "Charlie" won that round. If "Charlie" was around today I am sure, since after all he won, he would greet me with a smile and with that Vietnamese phrase, which we always used ironically, "Sin loi baby", "Sorry about that".And I am equally certain, that we would be friends.

Today, "Nam" has all but disappeared into the mists of time.

GLOSSARY
(The Language Of War)

Acronyms and euphemisms have always been a characteristic of military life. In fact it becomes a necessity, to save time and allow a rapid transmission of information. Unfortunately it also creates a barking staccato way of speech, using alphabet soup.

For example; "Company Headquarters B Company and the Intelligence Officer will Rendezvous at the Logistic Support Group Headquarters at 1.30pm for a Situation Report".
Translates to, "CHQ call sign 2 and the I.O. will RV at LSG HQ at 1330 hrs for a SITREP".
This becomes much more complex when euphemisms, nicknames, the phonetic alphabet and two-way radio procedure are used.

As the war grew in size and intensity so did the lexicon of the war in Vietnam. To the extent that by 1969, war speak was almost a dialect. The number of different names used to describe the Vietnamese, both North and South, enemy and friendly further complicated this.

There is a general acceptance that when soldiers are sent to fight and kill, it is necessary to create a good measure of hatred towards the enemy. Initially, this is normally done with a conscious first step to have a number of names with which degrade him, more often than not racially based.

This has been the case in every war in recent memory, where in the second world war for instance, the Japanese were called Japs, Tojo (from the emperor), Nips (from Nippon) While the Germans were Huns (an old tribal group from Europe) or Square Heads (the shape of their helmets)

The Korean war transformed the Chinese into Chinks.

In Vietnam a much more extensive list was developed, which sometimes had obscure derivations, such that a "Nog" (Nasty Oriental Gentleman), in the day time became a more sinister "Gook" (Spooky Gooky), at night time. In the last years of the war when it was obvious that the Vietnamese were winning, he was often referred to in a more respectful way as "Mr. Charles".

Another factor not encountered before, was the lack of clarity as to exactly who the enemy was, so that a civilian, North Vietnamese or VC could easily be described as a Dink, Slope or Fish Head. Obviously anything called NVA or Charlie was self-explanatory.

Some acronyms or slang have been omitted, as being used only by American forces or because they were rarely if ever used by Australian forces and would be out of out of context or difficult to understand.

This particularly applies to words, which have been used in films over the last twenty years, which has lead to words like "Nam", being used in place of Vietnam. In fact "Nam" is used most often by Australian "Bog Vets" or "Bogus Vets".

These Bog Vets, are found most frequently in pubs on Anzac Day. Telling stories of their time in "Nam", "Diddy Bopping" around the "DMZ", (Demilitarised Zone, in which the Australians never operated) "Zapping Gooks" by the hundreds. Finishing with "We lost a lot of good men out there" and a thousand yard stare, as the empty beer glass is nudged hopefully towards you.

NAMES USED TO DESCRIBE THE VIETNAMESE

Charlie	Shortened form of Victor Charlie.
Charlie Chan	Name of a detective from the old black and white movies.
Dinks	Their habit of "Dinking" two on a bicycle.
Fish Heads	Referred to their diet of fish heads and rice.
Gooks	More often used to describe night movement, like a spooky gooky.
Mr. Charles	Form of respect which came to be used after we lost.
NOGS	Nasty Oriental Gentlemen.
NVA	North Vietnamese Army. Regular
Slopes	Description of head shape.
Ruff Puffs	South Vietnamese regional and popular force soldiers.
Smacks	You know how you look after a "smack" in the face?
VC	Short for Viet Cong.
Victor Charlie	Phonetic alphabet used in radio procedure for the letters VC. Hence "Charlie"
Viet Cong	South Vietnamese guerrillas who fought for the North
V.Ns	General term for all Vietnamese.
White Mice	Vietnamese police dressed in white helmets and shirts with grey trousers.
Zip Heads	Vietnamese

OPERATIONAL ACRONYMS AND TITLES

AK-47	Lightweight Soviet or Chinese built 7.62mm assault rifle. Also known as the Kalashnikov. Still the guerrilla's weapon of choice today.

221

BUSHRANGER	Helicopter Gunship
CASEVAC	Casualty Evacuation, implying a combat injury.
COSVN	Central Office of South Vietnam The North Vietnamese Pentagon which never Really existed as a structure.
DMZ	Demilitarised Zone. The dividing line between North and South Vietnam along the 17th parallel
DONG	Unit of North Vietnamese money.
DUM DUM	A bullet modified to tumble or explode on impact.
DUSTOFF	Evacuation of wounded by helicopter.
FAC	Forward Air Controller.
FOO	Forward Observation Officer for artillery or mortars.
FREE FIRE ZONE	A designated area where anything moving could be regarded as enemy and be shot.
FRIENDLY FIRE	On the receiving end; it is never friendly.
FUBAR	Fucked Upped Beyond All Recognition.
FSB	Fire Support Base.
HOT EXTRACTION	Withdrawal of personnel, normally by helicopter whilst under enemy fire.
IRONSIDES	Radio designation for any armoured vehicle.
IROQUOIS (UH-1)	The workhorse helicopter of the Vietnam war. affectionately nicknamed Huey from its UH-1 id
JUMPING JACK	Land mine with a primary charge, which brings it to waist height, before a secondary charge sends shrapnel in all directions up to 300 metres away.
LZ	Landing Zone.
MACV	Military Assistance Command Vietnam.
MEDEVAC	Medical evacuation implying non combat injury
MPC	Military Payment Certificate currency used only by foreign military to dissuade the black market
PIASTRE	Old unit of South Vietnamese money.
POGO	Any troops not in the front line

POSSUM	Bell 47 helicopter capable of taking up to three passengers.
PUFF	The Magic Dragon. A DC3 aircraft fitted with 3 mini guns on each side, each capable of firing 6,000 rounds a minute
R & R	Rest and Recreation Leave also known as root and rave.
RECTUM RANGER	Member of armoured corps after a scandal during a training exercise.
SAPPER	Lowest ranking member of Engineer Corps.
SHELLDRAKE	Radio call sign for Artillery.
SITREP	Situation Report.
SLR	Self Loading Rifle. Standard issue Australian rifle.
SNOOPY	Another name for PUFF
SUNRAY	Radio call sign of any commander.
SUNRAY MINOR	Radio call sign of any second in command.
TET	Vietnamese / Buddhist new year
THE JASONS	Group of scientists created by US govt. to develop technology for military application.
TURD BURGULAR	Member of the battalion hygiene section.
TUCKER FUCKER	Any member of the Catering Corps

COMMON SLANG

Ba Mi Ba	(Viet. for 33) Local beer, still available today
CTD	Circling the drain or nearly dead.
Di Di	Go
Di Di Mau	Go Away
FNG	Fucking New Guy (US)
Ho Chi Minh Sandals	Sandals made from car tyres.
Long Timer	New arrival in country
PX	American Post Exchange (Supermarket)
Saigon Tea	A drink for bar-girls; supposedly whisky and ginger ale but more often than not just tea.

Short Timer	Nearing the end of the 12 month tour.
SOL	Shit Out Of Luck.
Zapped	To be shot.

ACKNOWLEDGEMENTS

There are many who gave their time and thoughts during the writing of this book and without whose encouragement it would never have been written. In particular I would like to thank John Neervoort, who was the platoon commander of the Trackers, for his unstinting support and ideas.

In the chapters on "Bright Ideas" I have used material and quotes from Greg Lockhart's excellent book The Minefield.

Thanks also to the members of the Tracker Platoon, 6RAR/NZ (ANZAC), 3 Squadron SAS, 3 Platoon, 6RAR/NZ (ANZAC) and of course Charlie, without whose participation none of these stories would have eventuated.

If there is a dedication, it is to the tracker dogs of the Vietnam War and those loyal Vietnamese Bushman Scouts.

The Bushman Scouts risked everything and whose fates will never be known.

The tracker dogs saved lives and, more importantly, our sanity. The wag of a tail and a lick on the hand was enough to make one smile in the most insane moment.

They provided the first sophisticated base, from which the military and civilian use of dogs was developed. We see the results every day. The various breeds, sniffing for mines in conflict zones, explosives and drugs at airports, or sniffing out people who have lost their way.

ABOUT THE AUTHOR

Percy Titchener was the result of a chance meeting and eventual marriage, at the end of the Second World War, between an Austrian opera singer and a New Zealand army Brigadier.

The family moved from New Zealand to India and lived there for eight years, enjoying the remnants of a very British colonial life style, which still existed in the early sixties. This was followed by a move to Australia to finish school and attend University.

However the Australian Army was very busy with a war in Vietnam and University was postponed. With the wisdom of a very naive seventeen year old, Percy joined the Australian Army as a private soldier. After serving in Vietnam in the infantry and being seriously wounded, he recovered and was eventually commissioned as a Lieutenant, into the cavalry (riding is better than walking).

The army was followed by several years struggling through a basic degree in biology, while at the same time completing a doctorate degree, in alcoholic beverages and exotic cigarettes. Over the last twenty-five years he has lived in Pakistan, West Africa, Italy, Croatia, Central Asia and South America. His interests are photography, languages and history. Today he divides his time between the Amazon in Brazil and Australia.